The Silver Scepter

~ Tales from Elderland ~

Book I

J.D. Mankowski

Published by J.D. Mankowski

2nd J.D. Mankowski Printing, September 2024
First Little Clocks Printing, May 2015
Copyright © 2024 Joseph McGovern

ISBN: 979-8-9918979-0-7

Printed in the United States of America
Cover Design by Dominic Critelli
Edited by Diane Shirk

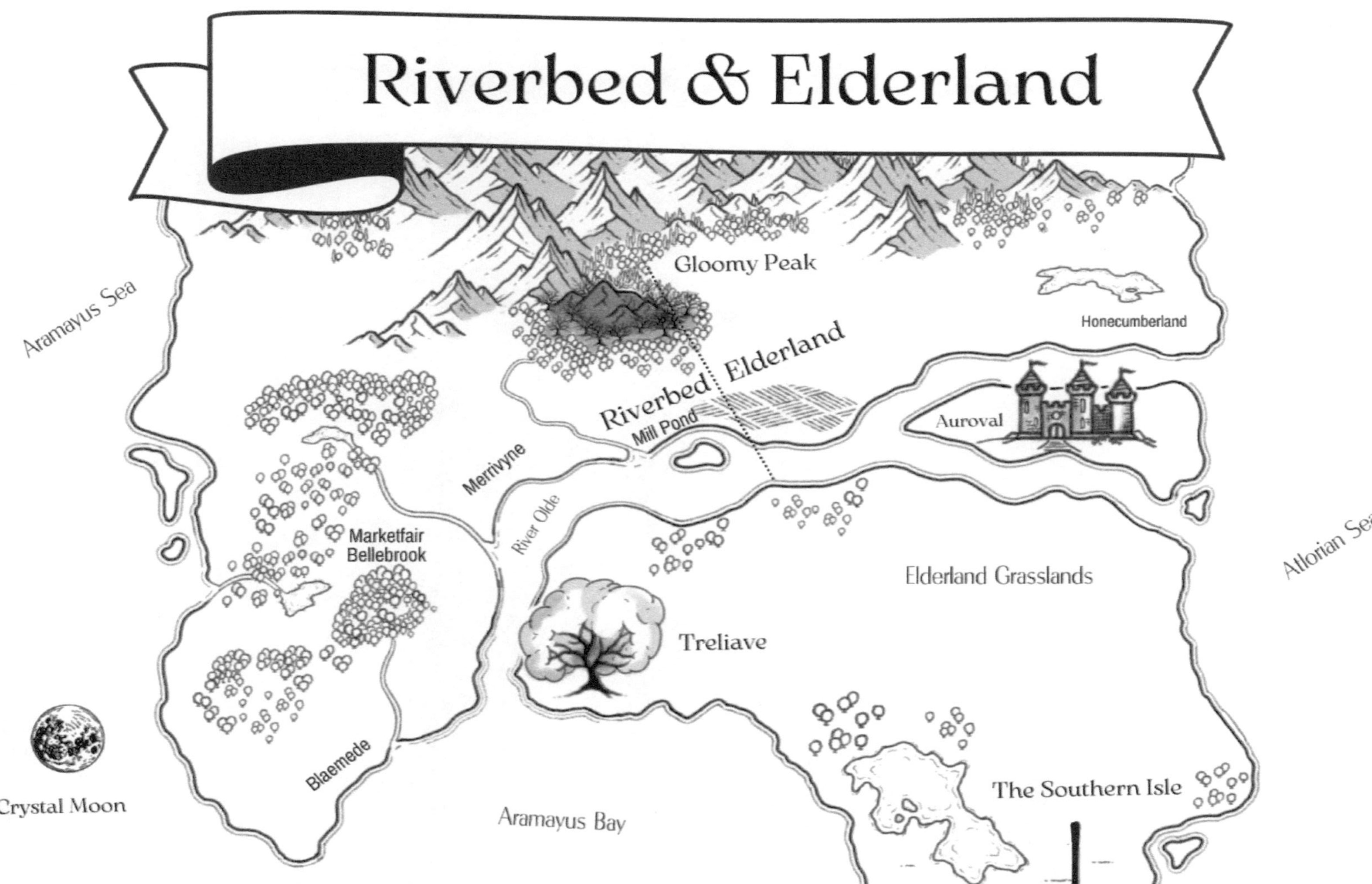

Riverbed & Elderland
Aramayus Sea
Gloomy Peak
Honecumberland
Riverbed Elderland
Mill Pond
Auroval
Merrivyne
River Olde
Marketfair
Bellebrook
Elderland Grasslands
Atlorian Sea
Treliave
Blaemede
Crystal Moon
The Southern Isle
Aramayus Bay

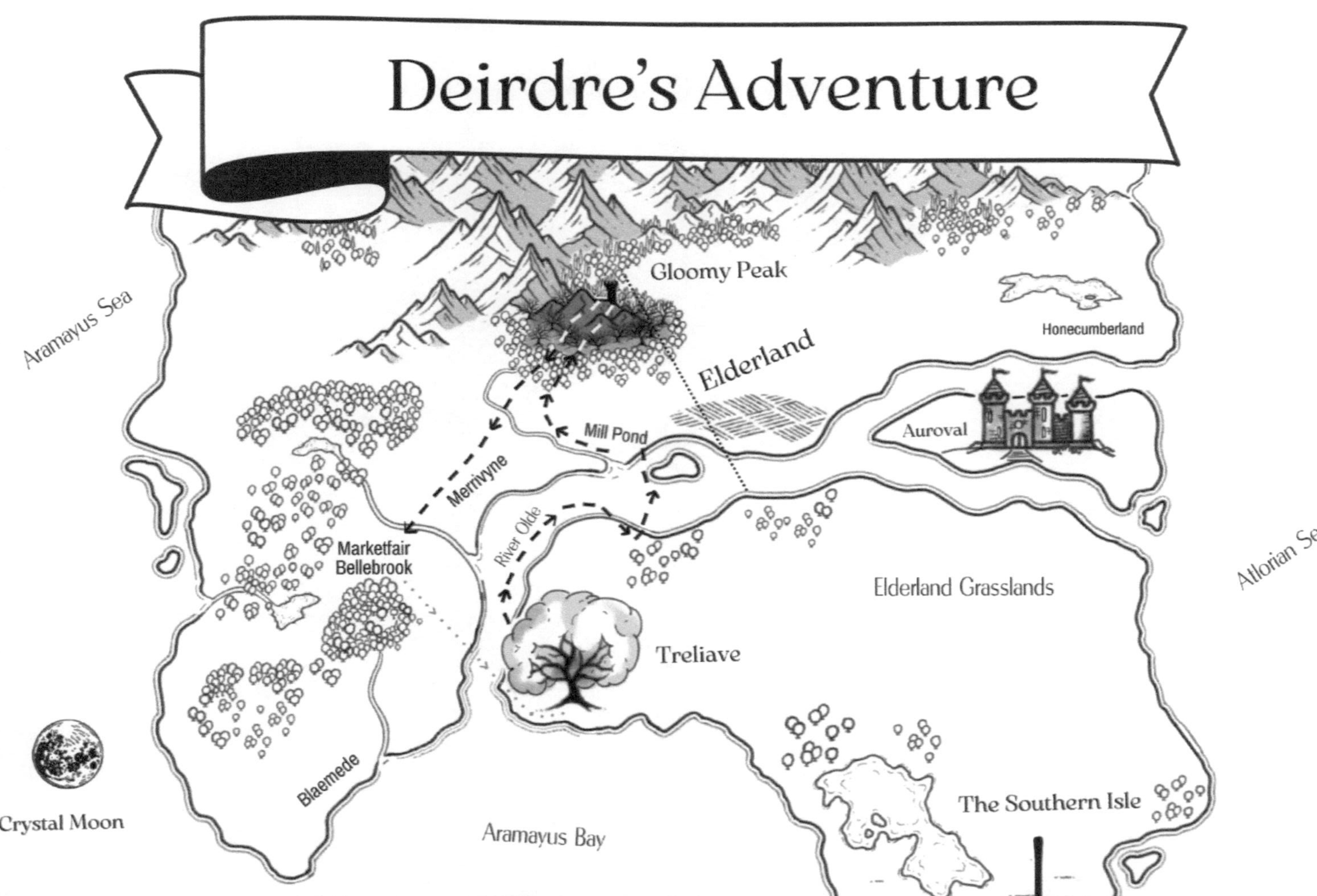

Deirdre's Adventure
Gloomy Peak
Honecumberland
Elderland
Mill Pond
Auroval
Aramayus Sea
Merrivyne
River Olde
Marketfair
Bellebrook
Elderland Grasslands
Attlorian Sea
Treliave
Blaemede
The Southern Isle
Crystal Moon
Aramayus Bay

-I-

THE HEART FAMILY

Little Miss Deirdre Heart, a proud eight-year-old tea party host with a vivid imagination, only ever asked her guests to please wipe their stuffed-animal paws before entering her cozy home constructed of blankets. This request became mandatory after Mr. Button, the bunny, insisted that the mud on his paws was merely a pair of new brown boots. Of course, nobody would have noticed this had not Woofus, the scholarly dog, barked at Mr. Button for refusing to pass over the chocolate chip cookies Madame Potbelle had made.

Appearances were everything to Deirdre, which was why she always had her blonde hair braided and held back by a purple ribbon. On Tea Party Days, she wore her favorite dress, which was white with lace trimming around the sleeves and skirt. A silver bow was tied around her waist and knotted against her lower back.

Being the host of the best tea party in Riverbed was a tedious title to uphold, to say the least. There were always guests to please, but according to the various stuffed animals owned by Deirdre Heart, nobody hosted a tea party better than her. The secret detail that set her above the rest was her paper doilies. Mrs. Heart had once told her, "If you wish for animals to behave themselves, give them something nice to place their teacups on." This was a secret kept between Deirdre and her mother. To the rest of her tea party guests, the doilies were made from the finest silk pollen could buy.

Our story begins in the early autumn season, when some of the leaves are still uncertain of what color to be, and the wind is only cold to those who choose to continue wearing their heatspell attire.

Mr. Heart was downstairs cleaning up the breakfast plates and whistling his usual cheerful tune while Pup, the family kitten, pawed at his ankles for leftovers. Upstairs in a bedroom painted yellow, Mrs. Heart looked around for her daughter.

"Deirdre, dear?" she called in mild confusion. Her daughter had been in the room only a moment ago.

"Mama, Mr. Button's jacket is missing a button," Deirdre exclaimed in reply as she trotted barefoot into the room. In one hand she held her stuffed rabbit by its ears, and in the other, there was a sewing kit she had run off to get. "He won't attend my tea party if he can't be dressed in his best."

Mrs. Heart kissed Deirdre on the forehead before examining the stuffed bunny. Aside from the pig that wore a tutu, Mr. Button was Deirdre's oldest stuffed animal. It had been dragged to Marketfair, the parks, the schoolhouse, and various neighboring yards. Mrs. Heart knew it had been only a matter of time before a proper stitching would be needed.

"Why doesn't he wear his blue jacket today?" Mrs. Heart prompted.

Deirdre mulled the suggestion over, but Mr. Button was adamant about looking his best. Theodore Bary III was attending today's tea party. He was Mr. Button's old rival. To be seen in his blue jacket when Theodore would most certainly be sporting a blue cashmere sweater would start competitive bickering about who was matching whom. This would be an argument Mr. Button would lose because Theodore only ever wore blue to Deirdre's tea parties.

"He won't wear it." Deirdre frowned as she looked from her rabbit back to Mrs. Heart.

"Ask him again," Mrs. Heart suggested, and so Deirdre looked at her stuffed animal for a second time. While the dilemma of tea party politics was being assessed, Mrs. Heart settled herself on a desk chair. She then beckoned Deirdre to pull a reading stool over so they could start painting her nails.

As Deirdre scooted herself closer, she watched as her mother reached towards a small pouch hanging by her waist. The pouch was made of white leather and could hold a fistful of marbles. Of course, Deirdre knew the pouch was not made for such a thing. It was for eldestree pollen. She watched her mother take a pinch of sparkling powder before sprinkling it over the sewing kit. The box sprang open. A faint cloud of white dust swirled around the contents of the kit. Spools of thread and needles began to float in the air. From the corner of her eye, Mrs. Heart looked at the one round button she had.

"We only have this yellow button," Mrs. Heart said.

As the big, yellow disc of wood floated closer to her hand, Deirdre examined the green tweed jacket Mr. Button preferred to wear. The yellow would not match the rest of the outfit. "I don't think he likes it," Deirdre said solemnly. "Yellow buttons or wearing blue today just won't do." She dropped Mr. Button on the floor and offered both of her hands to her mother.

Mrs. Heart smiled. "Well then, I guess we will have to look for the right button in Marketfair today."

Deirdre's eyes shot up with excitement. "We're going?"

"Mh-mm," her mother replied before dipping a little brush into a bottle. "We need to pick up a few things from Farmer Hutch's stand."

"And we can go to the Trinket Booth?"

Mrs. Heart nodded.

Deirdre paused. "But what if we don't have enough time for the tea party?" she asked.

"There's always time for tea parties!" Mr. Heart declared as he walked into the room. His eyes fell on the contents of the sewing kit floating gently in a swirl of white eldestree pollen.

"But we still have to bake cookies and sew a button onto Mr.

Button's jacket." Deirdre pointed towards the bunny on the floor. "And that's after we go to Marketfair."

"Don't move your hands," Mrs. Heart said as she applied the first layer of silver nail polish to Deirdre's pinkie fingers.

Scooping the stuffed animal off the floor, Mr. Heart said, "Well, why don't I just sew on a button now before we leave for Marketfair?"

"We only have a yellow one, and Mr. Button doesn't think it will go well with his jacket."

"And this is his best attire, isn't it?"

Deirdre nodded.

"Let me guess," Mr. Heart continued as he stared at the seventh chair situated around Deirdre's tea party table. "Theodore Bary is attending today's tea party, and that is why Mr. Button can't wear his blue jacket."

"Yes!" Deirdre exclaimed. Mrs. Heart gave her hands a gentle squeeze to ensure the nail polish didn't smear while looking at Mr. Heart in mild amusement.

"That ol' bear is always trying to bring competition to the table, isn't he?" Mr. Heart confirmed with Deirdre while examining the bunny's jacket.

Deirdre nodded.

Mr. Heart flicked his right middle and index finger. The faint wisps of pollen began to fade, and one by one the spools of thread and needles fell back neatly into the sewing kit.

"Thank you, darling," said Mrs. Heart.

Deirdre bobbed her head up and down while she watched her mother apply the second color of nail polish: green.

"Mr. Button is always jealous around Theodore. He says it's rude for the Duke of Honecumberland to travel during these strange times," Deirdre announced with such confidence and certainty that even she was a bit surprised by herself.

Mr. and Mrs. Heart exchanged a look Deirdre had never seen. It wasn't an angry look. Rather, it seemed closer to a stifled concern.

"We didn't know Theodore was a Duke," Mr. Heart said after a moment of silence.

Deirdre eyed her stuffed teddy bear when she replied, "I overheard Mr. Button discussing his frustrations with Woofus."

"Well, I wish we had known we were hosting a Duke," Mrs. Heart said. "I would have worn something a bit nicer."

Deirdre shook her head. "It's rude to discuss politics over tea. I think Mr. Bary was just trying to be polite by keeping it a secret." She glanced towards her tea party table. "But maybe we can add a few more flowers to the vase?"

Mr. Heart chuckled. "Good thinking."

"Can we pick some white pompoms?" Deirdre asked. She began to fidget with excitement, knowing they were her mother's favorite flower.

"No," Mrs. Heart said as she switched to the third color of nail polish: purple. "Let the pompoms be. They're the last of the season to be growing before frostforth returns."

"But they're your favorite!"

Mrs. Heart smiled. "Pluck a flower from its home and you may find yourself without your own," she warned while giving a playful tap on the tip of her daughter's nose.

Deirdre scrunched up her face and giggled. She watched her mother finish painting her nails with white and light blue. She hugged her mother happily and skipped downstairs to show Pup, not realizing that Mr. and Mrs. Heart remained in the bedroom to converse in softer tones.

When the sun had warmed the cobblestones, the Heart family left their home on Boxton Street. It was a quaint house, with dark window shutters and a thick wooden door. There were flowerpots and hanging baskets, which held lilies and mums. The trees, anticipating autumn, scattered their first leaves on a patch of grass in front of the house as gusts of wind rolled by.

A very disgruntled Deirdre stood at the bottom of the porch steps while her mother pulled two white mittens over her hands. "It's no longer heatspell, so you need to get into a habit of wearing them," Mrs. Heart said before ushering Deirdre along. After locking the door to the house, Mr. Heart laced his fingers between Mrs. Heart's, and they watched their daughter run ahead. Pup pawed at the window from inside — always curious as to why he was not brought on these family outings. His meows went unanswered.

Deirdre knew Bellebrook was one of five towns in Riverbed. She knew that on a map, it was located on the eastern bay of the Aramayus and that it was settled between the towns of Blaemede and Merrivyne. Bellebrook was known for its tidy streets, colorful homes, and for having a beautiful flower garden at its center. Blaemede was full of fishermen, ships, and orphans, and Merrivyne was known for its berry farms and spring-eve festival. She had never been to any of the other towns. But she had been to Marketfair, which hosted camping grounds for all the merchants in Riverbed and beyond. People from as far down the Great Road as Middleton and Mill Pond came to trade in Marketfair.

"Good morning, Hearts," called Madame Nancy from her porch as she peered over her spectacles.

"Good morning," Mr. and Mrs. Heart replied.

"My, oh, my. How quickly Deirdre seems to be growing."

Deirdre paused in her frolicking tracks, waved, and smiled at the comment.

"Yes," Mr. Heart said. "She's sprouting like a weed, isn't she?"

"A flower," Mrs. Heart corrected him. "Ladies grow like flowers. Boys grow like weeds."

Mr. Whitesal, Madame Nancy's husband, chuckled at the remark as he stepped out onto the porch. "Morning, Heart family," he said to them. In his hands, he held an accordion.

"Morning, Don," they returned.

"Off to the Marketfair?"

"That we are. Do you two need anything?" Mrs. Heart asked.

Deirdre skipped a little further down the road towards another familiar house. Sitting on the porch steps beside a pile of books and a bowl of water was Victriina Perkins. She was two years older than Deirdre but very shy, or so Deirdre had once overheard her parents saying to Mr. and Mrs. Perkins. Deirdre didn't think so.

"What are you doing?" she asked from the little gate at the edge of the street.

"Practicing," Victriina replied flatly. Her face was pressed into a look of severe concentration.

"Practicing what?"

"Calling."

Deirdre invited herself past the gate. "But only adults can call, and you need pollen to do it, not water." All the children in Riverbed knew that they had to wait until their sixteenth birthday to be given their own pouch of pollen. Mr. and Mrs. Heart had told Deirdre several times that it was too dangerous to be used by children her age. They promised that in time she would get to learn, but that day was still very far away.

"I saw a boy on the path by Pine Creek Bridge casting a silver cloud of pollen all on his own yesterday. He didn't even have a pouch," Victriina said. "And these books talk about a Pirate Queen who used to call the waters of the sea."

"It was probably a trick," Deirdre stated factually. Though it did not surprise her that a boy was playing with pollen in the woods. The boys in her schoolhouse were always getting into trouble. And yet, as Victriina wiggled her fingers and waved her hands at a bowl of water, Deirdre watched attentively, hoping that something might happen.

"What are you trying to make it do?" she asked.

"I don't know," Victriina replied as her face turned bright red. She let out a hefty sigh, then paused to move a lock of her hair away from her face.

"Deirdre, dear," her parents called. Both girls straightened their postures. Not wanting to get Victriina into any sort of trouble, Deirdre hopped off the porch and followed her parents' beckoning.

Bellebrook fell out of sight once the Heart family had stepped off its cobblestone road and onto a dirt-trodden path that slipped into a valley grove of trees. Further in was a lazy water trail. It babbled beside clusters of rocks and lapped ashore at a muddy divide where frogs preferred to play.

Mr. Heart paused halfway across what was known as Pine Creek Bridge. He closed his eyes and inhaled a great breath. "Smells like pine," he declared.

"Of course it does, darling. We're at the edge of town," Mrs. Heart replied with a smile as she and Deirdre continued ahead.

But Mr. Heart didn't move. "I'm serious."

"I know you are."

Deirdre had lost interest in her parents' strange conversation about the smell of pine and the "edge of town" as she caught sight of a large maple-looking leaf. This leaf was twice her size and too big to drift atop the water's surface. It was crimson with veins that shimmered like polished bronze.

"It would be silly to call it Pine Creek Bridge if the air smelled of cherry blossoms," Mr. Heart said before pecking Mrs. Heart on the cheek.

"You say this every time we cross the bridge."

"And I always will," Mr. Heart said before pecking her on the cheek a second, third, and fourth time. Noticing Deirdre's distracted gaze, he knelt beside her. "And do you know why, Little Dove?"

Deirdre partially kept her attention on the leaf and was thinking it would have made a wonderful setting for an outdoor tea party. She imagined her stuffed animals and tea set skillfully placed on top of the leaf in her backyard.

"Deirdre?"

Looking at her parents, she quickly replied, "Because life is about the small things." This was something her father reminded her of often, like when she helped him pick flowers for her mother, or when they looked at one of the moons before bed, or when she helped fold clothes.

"Look, darling," Mrs. Heart gasped. Her eyes had followed Deirdre's to the giant leaf. "An eldestleaf."

"What's an eldestleaf?" Deirdre asked.

The momentary bliss and wonder that had filled Mrs. Heart's eyes faded back into her standard mothering look — a mixture of love and overprotectiveness. She glanced at her husband, and they continued towards Marketfair.

"What's an eldestleaf?" Deirdre repeated.

"It's a leaf that belongs to a very old tree," Mrs. Heart said simply.

To Deirdre, however, this was not a time for simple answers. "What kind of tree?"

"An eldestree."

"That's where pollen comes from."

"Yes," Mr. Heart said.

"Do all eldestrees have eldestleaves like that?"

"No. Each eldestree is different, but an old Wayfarer once told me that they grew out of the sea hundreds and hundreds of years ago."

"Can we go see them someday?" Deirdre asked.

Both of her parents nodded, and Deirdre knew instantly that they were now telling only half-truths. The silent nod was always an indication that her mother and father were only saying as much as they needed to subdue the conversation. Recognizing this cleverness, Deirdre would have typically inquired for a little longer; how did an eldestleaf get here? How does one get pollen from an eldestree? Why weren't there any eldestrees in Bellebrook?

But in that same moment of gathering thoughts, Deirdre saw colorful banners and large crowds up ahead. The sound of auctioneers caught her attention. The Heart family had arrived at Marketfair.

-II-

FARMERS AND WAYFARERS

"Mill Pond grain, Mill Pond grain, freshest and finest in Riverbed!" shouted a vendor. "Aramayus peach-scales, caught last night and for sale by weight today!" shouted another. "Kazoos, Crackles, and Bursts of Glee, great for children of all ages!" exclaimed a particular vendor who made eye contact with Deirdre. "Even you, princess!" He wore a silly white top hat and a blue-tinted eyepatch. When she smiled at him, he tossed a small orb in the air and little fireworks erupted above his head.

Moving horse-drawn wagons, jugglers, fire-breathers, and the overbearing crowds of people forced Mrs. Heart to hold Deirdre's hand a little tighter than usual. Mr. Heart led them through the whirlwind of excitement towards the booths set aside for local farmers.

"Keep close," Mrs. Heart kept telling Deirdre as she gently pulled her along.

Deirdre nodded absentmindedly. It was impossible to see everything through all the movement. Deirdre strained her neck to catch glimpses of the thrills Marketfair had to offer. And although the Heart family only ever walked along the main avenue of booths,

Deirdre always looked for an area called the Narrows.

It was a menagerie of rainbow-colored tents and enclosed traveling carriages off the beaten path. The Narrows was operated by a group of traveling merchants known as Wayfarers. Deirdre had never been allowed in, which she found annoying because it was the most enchanting place she had ever seen from afar. The people in the Narrows looked funny in their oddly fitted petticoats and tunics. Some of them wore hats with feathers and little bouquets of seasonal flowers. The street performers with the most mesmerizing acts stayed near the Narrows' entrance. It reminded Deirdre of a carnival.

"Well, if it isn't my most loyal customers," announced Farmer Hutch happily as the Heart family arrived at his produce stand.

"How are you, Bucky?" Mrs. Heart asked kindly as her husband reached down for a wicker basket.

"I'm doing as good as always. I see the little lady is accompanying you!" He removed his wide-brimmed straw hat. "How are you, miss?"

"I'm well, thank you," Deirdre replied, beaming over the attention. "Your tomatoes look delicious."

Mrs. Heart had taught Deirdre that it was customary kindness to compliment a farmer on what they'd grown.

"Why thank you, miss," Bucky Hutch said and then laughed boisterously. "What can I get for you kind folks today?"

As the farmer's attention fell back towards her parents, Deirdre's attention returned towards the rest of Marketfair. She heard her parents request certain squashes and mushrooms. Intermittently, they asked for her opinion; Deirdre preferred sweet potatoes.

Eventually, however, her parents succumbed to adult small talk. Deirdre knew it'd be a long time before she'd get to pick out a button for her rabbit's jacket. She removed her mittens and placed them in her coat pockets, and after accomplishing that, she clasped her hands politely behind her back. Her eyes roamed aimlessly, failing to remain attentive to even Marketfair. She shuffled her feet, sighed to herself, and began drawing in the dirt with the tip of her right shoe.

It was only when her gaze fell between the ground and the produce stand's tablecloth that Deirdre saw a cat's tail wagging rhythmically back and forth. As Mr. Heart began to tell one of his favorite jokes, Deirdre politely tapped her mother's arm and asked to play with the kitten.

Mrs. Heart gave her a wink and nodded. Mr. Heart was well versed in small talk, whereas, like her daughter, she could only tolerate so much.

Deirdre lifted the cloth and hunkered under it to give the shy cat some well-deserved attention. Crouched in front of Farmer Hutch's feet, however, was not a cat. Deirdre had never seen a creature quite like it. It still had a feline figure, but its white fur was pristine to the point of shiny. Its snout was a smidge longer than that of a normal cat. And between its pointed ears was a pair of nubby charcoal-black horns. But what was most unmistakably different between this creature and her own Pup was that this creature had feathered wings.

Deirdre realized the eyes of this creature were like two marbles filled with churning oceans of ice.

From the depths of her captive mind, the word "Hello" fell from her lips. Carefully, she extended a hand to invite the animal closer. The creature casually obliged. It slipped beneath her open palm and purred in a chipper pitch. Deirdre giggled. Then the feline creature moved away in a slow and almost dignified manner.

"Where are you going?" Deirdre asked. She did not want to return to adult small talk. While she stared at the winged cat, Deirdre imagined she saw it blink just gently enough as if to invite her to follow.

Under any other circumstance, Deirdre knew better than to run off from her parents. However, when a mystical feline-creature as curious as the one Deirdre had found beckons, it felt equally rude to her not to follow. Deirdre assumed that somewhere within the hundreds of rules of politeness, there was a forgotten exception that allowed her to chase pretty animals through Marketfair. The feline creature slipped out from under Farmer Hutch's stand. Deirdre listened to Mr. Heart telling another joke. She reasoned that she would be back before he could even finish the punchline.

While dodging wagons and large crowds of people, Deirdre kept her eyes on the winged cat fluttering up ahead. It swooped and perched itself frequently enough for Deirdre to follow. In larger openings, it dropped to the ground and scampered about playfully. Deirdre was so enamored with the creature that she did not realize how far off she had wandered.

It was only when the winged cat darted behind a stack of wooden crates and barrels that she gave a second thought about finding her parents. But then the white-winged cat gave a distinctive trill and appeared between her legs. It purred loudly, caressing her ankles with the right side of its body. Deirdre bent over to pet it, but the creature slipped away again. It dodged and flew around her, causing her to spin into a spell of dizziness.

"Careful now, dearie," said a woman as Deirdre accidentally stumbled into an area of vibrantly colored awnings.

"Sorry," Deirdre replied absently. She had lost sight of the creature.

"Looking for anything in particular?"

Deirdre refocused her attention and found herself surrounded by four handcrafted carriages and a few merchant stands displaying potted plants, smoking pipes, and oddly assorted trinkets. The carriages themselves looked more like tiny traveling homes than means of transportation. They had little doors and windows, which faced into the gathering space. One carriage was painted sky-blue, the second a barn-red, the third was golden-sun yellow and the fourth a deep-evening purple. Their rooftops were made of sloped wooden shingles. Deirdre looked around as more people dressed in odd tunics and floral dresses appeared in the doorways.

"What are you looking for, dearie?" the woman asked Deirdre again.

Deirdre shook her head when words failed to come. Both her mother and father had warned her about going in the Narrows and begged her to never talk to strangers. Of all the strange people Deirdre had seen in Marketfair from a distance, this group of people was by far the strangest. The woman standing before her was old, with untamed black and pink hair, pale skin, and a piece of metal hooked through her left nostril. There was an excessive amount of jewelry hanging from her neck and wrists, not to mention the beads that were woven into her hair. A large leather belt tied around her waist held nearly a dozen pouches of pollen.

"Where are your mum and da'?" the woman asked.

"The-they're coming," Deirdre stuttered. She contemplated running away, but the other strangers from the four carriages moved in closer.

"Well, I think it's best you stay with us until they do. There are a lot of people who'd mistake you for an orphan and carry you south to Blaemede."

"I'll be okay."

The woman's lips spread into a rather repulsive grin. "Don't be silly. Come, come and see what we have to offer while you wait for your parents."

Deirdre glanced around as the other strangers continued to step closer. "Are you in need of a new stuffed bear, a pocket-sized pony, or dancing teacups?" asked the woman.

Deirdre shook her head, though she could not help but gawk at the thought of owning a set of dancing teacups.

"Perhaps you're more mature for your age. How about a tickling potion, a book of firetales, or a pollen pouch?"

"I'm too young to call pollen," Deirdre said quickly.

The woman smiled. "Of course, you are. Of course," she said apologetically. "And you're probably too young for these firetale stories." She moved around to another booth. "What about some marbles or buttons?"

Deirdre looked straight at the woman, saying all she had to without speaking a word.

"Marbles and buttons it is. Keep your feet there."

Deirdre had not moved an inch since she had stumbled into the woman. Fright had rooted her deep into the ground.

"What's your name, dearie?"

"Deir-Deirdre."

"Deirdre, what?"

"Deirdre," she sputtered. The group of merchants chuckled. Her parents had always warned her not to give her last name to strangers. Mr. Heart had even given Deirdre a false name to say in case a stranger inquired, but she was too scared to remember what it was now.

"Well Deirdre-Deirdre, my name is Vespra Rathmor," the woman said. She then pointed towards a stout man behind the smoking pipe booth. "That's Match Maksin." Her hand moved to a towering dark-skinned man. "That's Laz Reyson." And finally, her finger settled on a younger, prettier girl resting in a chair near the red carriage. "And that's Amalia Gift."

Deirdre imagined the girl would have stood closer like the others, but her foot was bent in an unnatural direction. Amalia looked like some of the older girls at her schoolhouse in Bellebrook — the type of girls that teased boys back.

"Nice to meet you," Deirdre said softly.

While reaching behind a booth, Vespra whistled a single note through her lips, and from inside the purple carriage came the white-winged cat. "You've already met my Pahlah, yes?" Vespra asked as Deirdre watched the creature flutter onto Vespra's shoulder.

Deirdre nodded.

"Have you ever seen a folisangel before?"

Deirdre's head shook in a different direction.

"Well, they don't typically inhabit the Riverbed towns." She walked over to Deirdre with a tray full of buttons of every shape, color, and size.

"I don't have any pollen," Deirdre confessed.

"No pollen?" Vespra gasped. "But what if you see a button you like?"

Deirdre looked back towards the long colorful alleyway for her parents. She wondered if they knew she was no longer under Farmer Hutch's booth. What would happen when they realized she was gone? Deirdre worried they might not find her, or that if they did, she would be in trouble. What if they canceled her tea party as punishment?

A few moments passed. Match disappeared into his carriage. Laz picked up a watering pail and began nurturing an assortment of exotic potted plants. Amalia continued sitting and staring at Deirdre.

"I'll tell you what, dearie," Vespra said cheerfully. "If you find a button you like, you can have it at the cost of one palm reading."

"A palm reading?" Deirdre repeated with uncertainty. "What's that?"

"You've never had your palm read?" Vespra said in the same shocked voice. She showed the inside of her own hand, tracing the lines and wrinkles to indicate that there was something to be said about them. "I can tell you who you are, and what futures lay ahead… if you fall in love with a handsome prince or a daring knight."

Deirdre looked at her own palms with a touch of skepticism. She'd seen her palms dozens of times and never knew they could tell her future. And if this woman was telling the truth, how come her teacher had never said anything at the schoolhouse? Or her parents at home?

"What pretty nails you have," Amalia remarked.

Deirdre could not help but smile. "I've had them painted for my tea party."

Vespra and Lazarus both laughed. "How charming," Lazarus said.

"Well, go on," Vespra prompted with a shake of her tray. "Pick something you like."

Deirdre took little to no time at all. Her eyes had already been sifting through the various colors of buttons. She scanned their shapes and sizes while thinking of her rabbit's favorite jacket. Her nimble fingers pinched a round, black button that had a polished white streak through its center.

"A perfect choice," Vespra praised. She placed the tray of beads and buttons behind her. Pahlah flew over to Amalia as Vespra knelt before Deirdre. "Are you ready to have your palm read?" she asked and waited for Deirdre to nod. "You can place your right hand in mine with your palm facing upwards."

Not knowing what to expect, Deirdre did as she was instructed. The group of Wayfarers no longer frightened her. In truth, she was quite fond of them. She even thought about inviting them to her tea party.

"I'll start with this line, your namesake line," Vespra began. "This tells me who you are, and who you'll be."

Deirdre felt the tip of one of Vespra's long nails slide over her hand. "You're eight years old, no siblings yet, but you have two loving parents…"

Deirdre looked up at the woman just in time to see her left eye change its appearance. Like Pahlah, Vespra's iris had become a swirling storm of blue, gray, and white. The nail on Deirdre's hand paused. Vespra said something out loud towards Laz in a tongue Deirdre had never heard before.

"That morning cup of tea must still be troubling your mind, Vezi," Laz replied after noticing Deirdre's inquisitive look.

"You're right," Vespra replied. She looked back at Deirdre. "Do you think your mum and da' will be here soon?"

Nodding slowly, Deirdre tried to mask her own worries. "What else does my palm say?" she asked.

At this, Amalia reached for a walking stick and stood. "I'll read her palm," she said while pulling her fire-red curls back behind her shoulders. Vespra accepted the offer, and Lazarus carried a stool over for Amalia. She thanked him.

"Ready?" Amalia then asked Deirdre with a gentle smile. When Deirdre confirmed that she was ready, Amalia began. "Oh, look here." She pointed at a line in Deirdre's palm but didn't explain. "Ah, and this one!" she exclaimed before falling silent for a long minute. "How interesting," she concluded.

Deirdre tried her best to hold still and wait patiently to be told about herself.

Eventually, Amalia looked up. Her gentle features helped settle Deirdre's nerves. "I see you surrounded by friends, tons and tons of friends, who admire and adore you. You're smart now, but you'll be even smarter in years to come. You'll have many adventures before you become a woman, and these adventures will lead you to your one true love.”

“Are you sure?” Deirdre asked quizzically. She was not certain how all this could be written on her hand.

“Of course, I’m sure,” Amalia said. “See these lines here?” She ran a finger along the two deepest creases running horizontally to each other. “The top one is your lifeline, and the second is your destiny. They’re in perfect alignment, which means nothing in your life is a coincidence. Everything that happens will happen for a reason. The little lines here by your thumb indicate how many friends you’ll have in life — and as you can see, there are a lot.” Amalia paused to watch Deirdre grin. “And that scar between your pinkie and ring finger… it looks like it came from climbing a tree?”

Deirdre nodded. She was impressed that Amalia could make such a guess. “There’s an apple tree behind my house that I fell out of last heatspell.”

“Well, there you go. A scar from an adventure that halts beneath your ring finger… adventures will lead you to your one true love.”

“Do both hands say the same thing?” Deirdre asked, but before any of the Wayfarers could answer, her mother’s voice called out from behind her.

“Deirdre!” she shouted in both anger and relief. “Deirdre, how did you get over here? What have we told you about running off?”

“I’m sorry,” Deirdre said as her face burned with embarrassment and shame. “I found Pahlah under the table and followed it here.” Deirdre pointed towards the folisangel perched on a chair.

Mr. Heart appeared a second later. “Little Dove, what were you thinking?” His eyes were much quicker to lift from where she stood to the surrounding carriages.

“We kept your daughter in good hands, Da,” Vespra ensured. “Don’t forget your button, dearie,” she then said to Deirdre while holding out the black and white button she had picked. Before Deirdre could retrieve it, however, Mr. Heart stopped her with an outstretched arm.

“She doesn’t need the button. Thank you for keeping her in your care." His tone was even but lacked real gratitude. Deirdre had never seen him so stern.

Vespra stepped forward. "But she purchased it. Foul trades bring misfortune to all."

At this, Laz agreed and said, "So claims the ceaseless tide."

"Darling," Mrs. Heart said softly as she knelt beside Deirdre to examine her inch-by-inch.

"How did she purchase it without pollen?" Mr. Heart asked.

"With a palm reading," Amalia explained.

Mr. Heart frowned. "Palm readings are not a form of currency."

"Not for you perhaps, but there can be great value in palms for us," Laz interjected. "And the reading wasn't finished."

"We don't mean any disrespect, but we will be leaving without that button."

As Deirdre was led away by Mrs. Heart, a loud crack and swirl of purple smoke forced them to stop in their tracks. Match Maksin appeared. "Foul trade!" he sneered. "Foul trade for us!"

Deirdre began to cry.

"Fine," Mr. Heart snapped. He withdrew his pouch of pollen, and from it he extended a pinch of white powder towards Vespra. "Accept this as compensation so no misfortune comes about."

Vespra moved swiftly about her alcove of merchant booths. She brought over a brass scale. In the right cup, she placed a pebble. Then she beckoned Mr. Heart forward. He rubbed his thumb and index finger together over the scale's left cup.

With two swift strokes, Vespra grabbed hold of Mr. Heart's hand and pried his fingers open. Her left eye changed back into its mystic swirl of ice as she pressed her thumb forcefully into the center of his palm. "Now the trade is fair," she said.

Mr. Heart retracted his hand and turned to see Match offering the button to Mrs. Heart. Vespra said something to her companions, and they all suddenly bowed.

"The truth will find you soon, Mum and Da." Her words were sharp with warning. "The Black Star will fall."

-III-

THE WINDSTONE

The Heart family left Marketfair quickly. Neither Mr. nor Mrs. Heart spoke as they followed the road back to the town of Bellebrook. They crossed the bridge without looking at the eldestleaf or commenting on the smell of pine. Deirdre knew it was not the time for questions, but she was concerned about this "truth" and "black star" business mentioned by the wayfarers. And why had all of them bowed at her parents? Of course, Deirdre had more sense than to ask about anything. Her father's stern behavior was enough reason to keep quiet and behave.

"To your room," Mrs. Heart said to Deirdre gently once they had arrived home. Before Deirdre made it to the staircase, Mrs. Heart extended a hand. "You can put this on your bedside with Mr. Button. I'll sew it on his jacket in a couple of minutes. Your father and I need to talk alone first."

"Am I in trouble?" Deirdre whimpered as she took the black and white button her mother had given her. Much like her status as the best tea party host, Deirdre's reputation as a well-behaved daughter meant the world to her.

"No." Mr. Heart sighed. "But do as your mother tells you."

Deirdre climbed the stairs up to her room. She placed the button next to her rabbit as instructed and carefully rearranged the napkins beside her paper doilies. Neither of her parents had told her whether the tea party would be canceled due to her behavior in Marketfair. If it were to be canceled, her guests would surely be disappointed.

Deirdre felt hot. She removed her autumn jacket. As it fell to the floor, Deirdre noticed one of her white mittens hanging out of a pocket. Both mittens had been tucked into her pockets while standing at Farmer Hutch's stand, but now only one remained. Knowing her mother would not be happy if she learned that Deirdre had lost one of her new mittens at Marketfair, Deirdre did the only thing she could think of. She shoved the one mitten she had under her bed. The guilt from being in the Narrows, the fear of what punishment had yet to come, and now the loss of her mitten sent Deirdre crying towards her bed. She sought comfort in her pillows and wished for such a horrible day to end.

Down in the kitchen, Mr. and Mrs. Heart continued their private conversation. Mr. Heart was tidying up the already clean room as Mrs. Heart spoke.

"I just don't believe it was a coincidence," Mrs. Heart said. Her arms were folded while she leaned against the kitchen table. "One of Treliave's leaves drifting all the way to Riverbed. The chances of that happening are essentially…"

"Zero. An eldestleaf would have had to drift against the incoming frostforth winds," Mr. Heart agreed.

"And those Wayfarers… the folisangel… how did they get to Deirdre so quickly?"

Mr. Heart shook his head and sighed. "So long as we stay in Bellebrook we can only guess, but I fear staying is no longer an option."

Mrs. Heart wrapped her arms tighter around herself. Her eyes drifted towards the kitchen window; outside she could see a little garden and apple tree in the back of their property. "I knew you were thinking that while we were walking back. I don't think we should act so quickly."

"We will talk to Woodrow and the others first," Mr. Heart said as calmly as he could. He pulled his wife into a warm embrace. "Will fall," he muttered. "The Wayfarer said the Black Star will fall, not that it already has. There is still time."

Before Katherine could respond to her husband, something above thumped across the floor. They both looked up.

Deirdre, at that same moment, lifted her head from her tear-stained pillow. The door to her bedroom was ajar, and out in the hallway, she saw a trail of orange yarn on the floor. The ball itself bounced down the stairs. A second thump and dizzied meow indicated that Pup had gone with it. Deirdre tiptoed out of her bedroom to see her kitten tangled in a heap of yarn at the bottom of the first-floor landing.

"Mischievous," Mrs. Heart said to Pup before looking up at Deirdre. "How about we start baking cookies for the tea party?" she asked with a type of healing smile that only a mother could give.

The Heart Family's mood wasn't restored that afternoon, but Mrs. Heart tried her best to settle Deirdre's worries. While she helped fasten the new button to Mr. Rabbit's jacket, Mr. Heart helped Deirdre elevate the roof of her blanket fort so that everyone could sit comfortably beneath it.

"All set, Little Dove?" Mr. Heart asked once Deirdre had finished placing her stuffed animals in their designated chairs.

She nodded and took her own seat. Each guest held a hand of the person (or paw of a stuffed animal) next to them before closing their eyes. "Sors, Sove, Advi, Reign," Mr. Heart said firmly.

A tickling sensation rolled through Deirdre's body. She kept her eyes closed, obeying the rule her parents made her promise to always follow. Only when one of her tea party guests spoke was she allowed to then open her eyes. Deep down, Deirdre knew her parents were using pollen. She was not supposed to know, but one time she broke her promise. It had only been for a half of a split second. In between her fluttering eyelids, she had once seen sparkling white clouds swirl around the entire tea party table. It was one of the most beautiful moments Deirdre had ever experienced, or rather not experienced. It was as if she had been caught in a freshly shaken snow globe.

This, of course, was the most exciting moment of the tea party for Deirdre. She was never sure which of her stuffed animals would speak first. On this particular day, it was Mr. Woofus. "Goodness me, did I get the time wrong?" the stuffed dog inquired in a low growling voice. He was peering at a timeteller, which he had pulled out from his little brown overcoat. Deirdre opened her eyes to see the other stuffed animals beginning to fidget.

"No, no, you're simply the first one here," Deirdre told him as he settled more comfortably into his seat.

Not a minute later Madame Potbelle, who was wearing a string of pearls with her white tutu, spoke cheerfully, "Good to see you, sweetie."

Mr. Button awoke with a shake of excitement. "Something smells delicious!" he declared while rubbing his paws together.

"Something smells truly marvelous," Theodore Bary boomed.

Mr. Button looked away as if not to notice the brown stuffed bear and took an interest in polishing the new button on his jacket.

"Thank you," Deirdre replied.

"Heart family, it is lovely to see you again," Theodore said.

"We're glad you could make it," Mrs. Heart replied as he shook the bear's paw.

"Mrs. Heart, you appear as radiant as ever!" Woofus remarked as he looked up from his timeteller.

"You're too kind, Woofus," Mrs. Heart said. "Busy in the archives?" she then asked the dog. "Last we spoke, you were researching the whereabouts of certain artifacts for our neighbors."

Deirdre did not recall this conversation happening at her last tea party. She hadn't even been aware of the fact that Mr. Woofus was doing research for the Whitesals, or maybe it was for Victriina Perkins's parents? Deirdre nodded and played along with the conversation. Woofus was, after all, a scholarly dog. Further still,

Deirdre knew better than to be a nosy host, so she sat back quietly and listened.

"Busy in the archives, indeed," Woofus said. "They've been very particular about recovering a specific heirloom for Kenan. A staff that had originally been given to Aria."

Mr. Button tapped Deirdre with a padded paw. "What is that delicious smell?" he asked her quietly.

"Homemade chocolate chip cookies. They should have cooled off enough by now to serve if you'd like one?"

Mr. Button's eyes shimmered with delight. "I most certainly would."

Deirdre nodded with a polite smile. There was no point in entertaining her guests since Woofus had taken the lead on conversing with Mr. and Mrs. Heart. With careful movements, she moved around the table and poured tea into each cup before leaving the room to fill a plate with cookies from the kitchen. In the end, Deirdre's tea party concluded as another success.

As evening settled into night, a luminous orange glow pushed through the drawn window curtains from inside house number sixteen on Boxton Street. The dinner dishes had been cleaned, the tea party cups were returned to their special cabinet, and Mrs. Heart had finally finished rewrapping another ball of yarn as Mr. Heart made his way upstairs.

"Final countdown before story time," he announced. "Five," he counted; the clinking of a toothbrush being dropped into a glass jar echoed from the washroom. "Four." The pattering of bare feet on wooden floors sounded as a blur of blonde hair came rushing down the hall. "Three." That same pair of feet jumped off the bedroom floor and into bed as Mr. Heart stepped into the doorway. "Two." He chuckled, watching his rampant daughter toss pillows around and yank at blanket corners to make room for her own wriggling. "And one," Mr. Heart concluded as Mr. Rabbit was pulled by the ears from a nightstand and wrapped into Deirdre's arms.

"All snug as a bug in a rug?" Mr. Heart asked.

Deirdre nodded, unable to suppress her excitement. She loved bedtime stories. Occasionally, Mr. Heart would allow Deirdre to choose the tale. She had her favorites; *Greenie the Giant*, *The Pirate Queen and her Flying Ship*, or *The Silver Sword of Atloria*. Some stories were about princes saving princesses, and other times there were princesses saving princes. Deirdre was certain there wasn't a story in the world her father didn't know, and so rather than waste time trying to decide on one she wanted to hear, Deirdre only offered silent nods to each of her father's questions.

"Teeth scrubbed?" he asked, and she nodded. "Hair brushed? Dirty socks placed in the basket? Is Mr. Button being hugged just right?"

Deirdre nodded, and nodded, and squeezed her rabbit.

"Well then, tonight I have a very important story for you."

Deirdre waited.

"Unless you'd rather just go to sleep," Mr. Heart teased.

"Tell it," she demanded.

Seating himself on the edge of her bed, Mr. Heart let out a long yawn and stretched. He playfully collapsed on top of Deirdre, and she laughed helplessly.

"Tell it!" Deirdre squealed.

"All right, all right," Mr. Heart said.

Deirdre nuzzled herself beside her father while holding Mr. Button close.

"There are four eldestrees in the world," Mr. Heart began. "The eldestleaf you saw today belongs to an eldestree named Treliave, and the Pine Creek Bridge we crossed on our way to Marketfair is made from another Eldestree, Raknaan. As far south as the Wayfarers can travel stands Muradescent. And to the east, where the great city of Auroval stands, is where the eldestree, Auro, resides." He paused to see if Deirdre would interrupt with a question, but she only nodded with widening eyes. "Every eldestree is unique in its own way, with long histories and many miraculous tales. Far too many to fit into one bedtime story, so tonight I will tell you about Auro."

Mrs. Heart entered the bedroom. She leaned against the doorway to listen.

"Auro is the smallest of the eldestrees but by far the mightiest. He is also the most important of the four because he chooses who becomes a Sovereign of Elderland. You would recognize his pollen, Little Dove. It's as white as freshly fallen snow."

"He?" Deirdre interjected. "Are they all boys?"

"No," Mrs. Heart replied. "Treliave and Muradescent are women."

"How?"

Mr. Heart chuckled. "A story for another time."

Deirdre wriggled back into her covers. Bedtime story rules dictated that all questions were supposed to be held until the end.

"Auro was founded by the first Sovereigns of Elderland hundreds of years ago. He was situated alone on an island of his own making. High upon a hilltop, his presence shimmered like a giant jewel. The founders decided to start a beautiful city around the eldestree for all who traveled to see it. As word spread of the miraculous eldestree, pirates with their ships tried to come and steal it. The castle of Auroval was built around Auro to protect him. A great warrior princess, whose story you already know, was Auro's most famous defender. And when peace finally came to Auroval, Auro's greatest gifts were bestowed upon his people.

Every morning, Auro blossoms with thousands of white petals. And at midday, servants of the castle in Auroval catch them with glass cauldrons as they fall. Little leaves of sterling silver and bright pink unfurl from Auro for the remainder of the day. Each one catches the sunlight and refracts small rainbows around the atrium where Auro resides. By sunset, the petals that have been collected in cauldrons wither into white pollen for us to use, but the ones that are not caught are left on the floor. At midnight, the silver and pink leaves wilt so the cycle can repeat itself. But every now and then a white petal on the floor is covered by a fallen leaf, and on nights when the Crystal Moon takes to the sky, its silver glow transforms the petal and leaf into a mystical little treasure known as a windstone."

Mr. Heart reached into his pocket and produced a smooth, egg-like piece of glass. "This is one of them," he said with a smile. "Under the light of the moon, it will glow pearl-white like the pollen Auro gives, but under the light of the sun, it will sparkle like a diamond."

Deirdre stretched her hands out for it, but rather than placing it in her palm, Mr. Heart blew gently on the windstone. Like a feather, it rose several inches above their heads and hovered.

"If you breathe on the stone and think of someone you love, the wind will scoop it up and take it to them. Your mother and I want you to always carry this with you when you leave the house, Little Dove. We want you to keep it safe, and should you ever feel lost, blow on it and think of us. The windstone will come to us, and we will know in which direction to find you."

Carefully, Mr. Heart guided Deirdre's hands beneath the stone. "Promise to keep it safe?"

"I promise," Deirdre replied. Slowly the stone fell into her open palms. The windstone was as hard as a rock, but as weightless as the petal she imagined it had been made from. She grinned brightly.

"We love you," Mrs. Heart said.

"Good night," Mr. Heart concluded.

Both of Deirdre's parents kissed her on the head.

As Mr. Heart snuffed out the candles in her room, Deirdre placed the stone on her nightstand. Once alone, she listened to her parents' footsteps as they traveled downstairs. Only when she felt it was safe did she tiptoe to her window and shift the curtains until a sliver of moonlight stretched across her bed. Back at her nightstand, Deirdre then positioned the windstone so that it could catch the light. It began to glow just as her father had said it would. Deirdre placed her head on her pillow and studied the swirls and plumbs of white lights churning within her new gift. Her eyes grew heavy. Thoughts of Auro, Altaa the Warrior Princess, and Auroval melded into a line of possible dreams. Then, all at once, Deirdre lost focus and went to sleep.

-IV-

UNEXPECTED GUESTS

Deirdre slid out of bed and headed downstairs for breakfast. Her windstone remained on her nightstand — dazzling in the new daylight.

"Deirdre, dear," began Mr. Heart as he washed a frying pan, "your mother and I will be gone for the evening. Madam Nancy and Mr. Whitesal will be coming over to look after you."

Deirdre frowned silently at this announcement. Typically, her father and mother planned their evenings away from her ahead of time. This was a family rule Deirdre had made, for there had once been a time when her parents forgot to RSVP "no" to her High Sociotea Party. All the guests were wondering where Mr. and Mrs. Heart had been, and as any tea party host knows, an empty seat at the table is an insult to the host. Deirdre poked at a breakfast sausage.

"Madam Nancy and Mr. Whitesal will fill our spots at the tea party tonight," Mr. Heart promised.

Deirdre nodded but refrained from offering any form of eye contact. Woofus was going to talk about his research tonight. Deirdre had assumed her father would want to be around for this conversation, but apparently not. "Where are you and Mama going?" she finally asked.

"We are going to meet some old friends outside of town."

Deirdre recognized her father's half-truth. She knew all of Mr. and Mrs. Heart's friends; her parents were always hosting dinners and small gatherings at the house. If they had been meeting friends, Deirdre knew her father would have named them. He would have said, "We're going to be with the Perkins," or "we're having dinner with the Kerns." Beyond this observation, Deirdre had also tuned into the vagueness of "outside of town." It was rare that Deirdre's parents ever left Bellebrook, and when they did, they always left a name and place for her and the Whitesals.

"Will you be home in time to tuck me in?" she asked.

Mr. Heart placed the frying pan on a hook above the stone. "Sorry, Little Dove. I'm afraid we won't be back in time for that."

The front door opened and then quickly closed. Mrs. Heart called out to them from the main foyer as she removed her coat. "The Perkins are willing to lend us their carriage and driver, Richard. I told you all we had to do was ask."

"That you did," Mr. Heart called back. "What time will their driver be picking us up?"

"No later than four, if we are to make good timing," Mrs. Heart said a little softer as she approached the kitchen. "Good morning, you," she then said warmly to Deirdre before giving her a kiss.

"Your nose is cold!" Deirdre said.

"Autumn is finally here," returned Mrs. Heart.

Mr. Heart locked eyes with Pup, who was creeping into the kitchen with ravenous breakfast-eyes. As Mrs. Heart sat down before her own plate of food, Pup trotted over to his empty food bowl and nudged it with his nose. When Mr. Heart refused to feed the cat scraps, Pup meowed.

"Deirdre, did you forget to feed Pup?" Mrs. Heart asked.

"No, he already ate." Deirdre frowned at the kitten; he was putting her good name into question.

"I watched her feed him," Mr. Heart attested as Pup meowed again.

The crafty kitten pawed the bowl closer to him.

Mrs. Heart watched with a coy smirk. "He's behaving rather silly, isn't he?"

"That he is," Mr. Heart said quickly. He broke eye contact with the kitten and moved over to the table. He kissed Mrs. Heart. "Deirdre's right. Your nose is cold!"

"I've been telling you both for weeks now that autumn is coming, and now it is here. Heatspell is over," Mrs. Heart said with her typical mothering assertion. "Which reminds me, Deirdre, whatever happened to your white mittens?"

This question hit Deirdre like a bucket of ice water. She quickly stabbed the sausage with her fork and forced it into her mouth. She garbled something along the lines of "coat, bedroom, safe" before swallowing, to which her mother replied, "Please don't talk with your mouth full."

Deirdre nodded quickly.

"And be sure to bring those mittens downstairs. They belong in the coatroom, not your bedroom," she added.

"Yes, Mama," Deirdre answered.

"I'd like to see them before your father and I leave."

Before the conversation could continue, Mr. Heart let out a yelp.

Pup had appeared in midair. He had leapt from one of the countertops behind the kitchen table, toppling into view. Cups of juice and milk sloshed to the floor, and the centerpiece broke — spilling flowers into everyone's laps. Pup stopped tumbling just in time to plant his face into the remains of Deirdre's scrambled eggs.

"PUP!" Mr. Heart hollered. Before the kitten could scamper away skittishly, he was yanked by the scruff of his neck and taken towards the coatroom.

"Silly Pup," Deirdre said to her mother in hopes of diffusing any tension.

"Silly Papa," Mrs. Heart answered smugly while picking flower stems and petals off her lap.

Throughout the remainder of the morning and early afternoon, Deirdre kept herself occupied with a game of "Hide from the Queen." It was a game she played whenever her mother was in an ordering mood. Mrs. Heart often rolled off lists of reminders and chores whenever Deirdre passed her field of vision.

"Don't forget to make your bed," or "Remember to pick up your socks," or, today's specific topic, "Don't forget to bring those mittens downstairs."

Mr. Heart had indirectly taught Deirdre this game. She had once caught him sneaking about the house one afternoon. And after asking him very pointedly what he was doing, Mr. Heart had told her he was hiding from the Queen. That was when Mrs. Heart rounded the corner of the living room and asked him if he would de-weed the garden.

Sometimes, as Deirdre had learned, Mrs. Heart would use specific hallways around the house so her daughter could hear her clearly when she shouted a reminder. It was important to be far from those specific echoing halls.

The game was not for the faint of heart. Every step around the house had to be made with accurate foresight. When the old grandfather clock in the main foyer chimed a quarter to four, Deirdre claimed victory and skipped into her bedroom for the first time that day. Not more than a minute later, Mrs. Heart called out to her, "Deirdre, dear, come down and say goodbye."

Deirdre glanced at her tea party table and smiled. The teacups and saucers were already set. Having not set them in place herself, she could only guess it had been done by her father, who had definitely noticed her "Hiding from the Queen" behavior.

Hurrying back downstairs, the first thing Deirdre noticed upon seeing her parents was that they were dressed in odd clothing. Mr. Heart looked like Woofus in a dark gray vest and jacket she had never seen before. His typically scruffy face was now cleanly shaven. And Mrs. Heart, who had always looked her best, was now dressed like the women of royalty mentioned in Deirdre's bedtime stories. Dark satin fabric fell in elegant folds around her. Silver and white pieces of jewelry hung from her ears, neck, and wrists. As Deirdre planned to ask again about where her parents were going, a brisk knock sounded from the door.

"Nancy and Dom don't have a coachman," Mr. Heart said as he glanced through one of the windows by the door.

Mrs. Heart smoothed out a few wrinkles in her shawl. "The Perkins' driver said he'd arrive at four," she said.

Although suspense held the Heart family in silence as Mr. Heart pulled open the door, relief was not what Deirdre felt when she saw who had knocked.

"Hello, Mrs. Doris," said Deirdre's mother with a touch of confusion.

"Dom's bedridden with some sickness. Nancy sent her gardener to me this morning to ask if I could watch the child," said Mrs. Doris promptly. She shoved herself through the doorway before either Mr. or Mrs. Heart could invite her in.

"Thank you for doing so on such short notice," Mr. Heart said as kindly as he could.

To Deirdre, this was most unfortunate news. Nancy and Dom were supposed to be the honored guests at her tea party. Mrs. Doris was an old hag, a word Mr. Heart used frequently to describe Mrs. Doris but always made Deirdre swear not to repeat such foul talk.

Mrs. Doris was like all old people, almost. She wore a gray wig, big glasses, and a never-ending assortment of floral clothing. However, instead of smelling like perfume, Mrs. Doris smelled of rotten cabbage, and instead of smiling, Mrs. Doris expressed a permanent frown. Mrs. Doris was not one to participate in tea parties. She said tea made her insides turn. Deirdre never learned what the tea turned Mrs. Doris's insides into, but she assumed it was something just as foul as regular, grumpy, old Mrs. Doris.

"You're a few minutes early," Mrs. Heart admitted. "The coachman should arrive soon."

"I say if you're early, you are on time. If you're on time, you are late, and if you're late, don't bother showing," wheezed Mrs. Doris.

Deirdre secretly wished Mrs. Doris had been late. Upon seeing Pup scampering through the halls, the old woman barked at Mr. Heart to chase after the kitten and lock him in a room. Deirdre felt sorry for Pup; this was the second time in one day he had been restricted to the coatroom.

After Pup had been locked away, Mrs. Heart informed Mrs. Doris that Deirdre had not been fed supper.

"My fingers are too stiff to cook. I hired a house assistant for myself months ago," snapped Mrs. Doris.

Mr. Heart grumbled that he'd prepare a small fire in the stove and warm some soup and moved towards the kitchen.

Deirdre followed him. She could hear him muttering under his breath. It felt wrong, seeing her father so agitated. Deirdre preferred her father to be his typical smiling self. While she shadowed him, a thought struck her. "How does the Aramayus say hello?" Deirdre asked him.

"Pardon?" Mr. Heart replied.

"How does the Aramayus say hello?" Deirdre repeated.

Mr. Heart lit the stove and began searching for some jarred soup. He scrunched up his face, letting the excitement in Deirdre's eyes build. "I don't know, Little Dove."

"It waves," she answered with a triumphant smile.

Mr. Heart laughed. "Of course, it does," he said and pulled her beneath one of his burly arms.

As dinner was warmed, Mrs. Doris plopped down into one of the armchairs in the gathering room, only to give Mrs. Heart an earful about how this particular armchair always gave her backaches. "I usually don't do these sorts of things out of the blue, Katherine," Mrs. Doris said. "If Nancy wasn't such a good friend, I would have never agreed to this. I hate children, all children, though I'm sure you know this. They don't sit well with me, and they never have. Just today I saw one running amok through the streets like a wild pig. He was covered in mud. Laughing boisterously. Looking through windows like a little criminal. I was in half-a-mind to tie him to the nearest lamppost. It's a shame the jailhouse doesn't hold children younger than twelve. But Nancy swears your little one has been raised right. I don't recall having an issue with her the last time I watched her. Though as I am sure you know — children are unpredictable."

When the old hag finally paused to breathe, a wave of relief washed over both of Deirdre's parents. "The coachman's here," Mr. Heart said quickly, appearing from the hallway.

Mrs. Heart knelt before Deirdre. "Be good," she said. "Be respectful to Mrs. Doris. Go to bed on time. Clean up after your tea party. Brush your teeth, and —"

"Never forget that you love me," chimed in Deirdre.

"Exactly," Mrs. Heart said with the warmest of smiles. She kissed Deirdre on the cheek. "And don't forget to bring down your mittens before bed."

After watching her parents roll down the street in the Perkins' horse-drawn carriage, Deirdre lingered in the entryway of the gathering room. She greeted Mrs. Doris as sweetly as she could. "Hello, Mrs. Doris. How are you today?"

The woman grunted an incoherent response. As usual, Mrs. Doris had dropped her serpent-scale bag beside the armchair. She pulled out an ugly, pea-green, tangled ball of yarn that was supposedly a scarf.

"Would you like to attend my tea party?" Deirdre asked, trying to be as kind as possible.

Mrs. Doris grunted a flat, "No."

"Can I get you a glass of water?" Mrs. Heart always told Deirdre to be a good hostess to house guests, even if they were only there to watch over her.

Peering over her thick, brown glasses, Mrs. Doris said sharply. "Do you remember my three rules?"

"Don't bother you, don't speak to you, don't stand anywhere that you can see me unless I'm in trouble."

"And why is that?"

"Because adults are happiest in silent, empty, child-free spaces."

The exchange of words was the only conversation Deirdre and Mrs. Doris ever had.

The old woman grunted a third and final time, and Deirdre understood it to be the sound of approval and dismissal. So, not caring to stay around any longer, Deirdre quietly walked back up to her room and closed the door.

Once safely concealed within her room, Deirdre positioned her stuffed animals in their designated seats. She removed the two extra chairs and carefully tucked them out of sight; the last thing she wanted was for her guests to wonder over those who were not attending. Then, after meticulously adjusting her tea set, Deirdre took her own place beneath her fort of blankets.

Without Mr. Heart to use pollen at the table, Deirdre knew the responsibility fell to her. She knew she wasn't supposed to, but her guests were depending on her. Copying her mother's tendencies, Deirdre smoothed the wrinkles out of her own tea party dress. Then she grabbed Mr. Woofus's left paw and Madame Potbelle's right hoof. She closed her eyes and whispered, "Sors, Sove, Advi, Reign."

She waited. At first, she was filled with patience. Her posture was held beautifully straight. Her eyes remained shut. Deirdre waited a whole minute before she felt as though the words had not worked. "Sors, Sove, Advi, Reign," she repeated with a touch more assertiveness. Then she waited again, but with less patience. Her posture remained straight, but she struggled to keep her eyes shut. Deirdre waited a whole thirty seconds before peeking at her guests. To her disappointment, her stuffed animals were still sitting stiffly in their seats.

"Sors, Sove, Advi, Reign," Deirdre said in a flustered tone. She squeezed the paws in each of her hands, closed her eyes up tight, and repeated the phrase again and again and again. But nothing happened. Nothing changed. Deirdre sat alone in her room realizing that without pollen, no one would be attending her tea party tonight. Her title as the Best Tea Party Host would surely be passed on to someone else.

Deirdre looked towards Madame Potbelle, who was also a tea party host. The longer she stared at her stuffed pig, the more Deirdre began to see a faint smirk of satisfaction curling beneath Madame Potbelle's pink snout. Her beaded black eyes now looked as though they were made to sabotage a tea party. Deirdre felt rude accusations crawl onto her tongue when, suddenly, from the corner of her room, she heard a loud *thump*.

Turning around, Deirdre expected to see Mrs. Doris standing in her doorway, but the bedroom door was still closed. Deirdre remained seated at her table. She looked around her yellow room — scanning the furniture, neatly hung clothes, and decorative pillows. As her gaze hovered somewhere between the bed and window, a second thump sounded.

From down below Mrs. Doris hollered, "Children are not to be heard!" And with this, Deirdre knew it wasn't just her and Mrs. Doris in the house.

"Hello?" Deirdre whispered, and in response came a third, fourth, and fifth *thump, thump, thump*. The noise came from the window and scared Deirdre out of her seat. Mrs. Doris shrieked something for a second time, but it was lost in the non-echoing hallways as Deirdre crept towards her window.

The shutters, Deirdre rationalized, were just rattling in an autumn breeze. And for a moment this made sense to her as she opened and peered out her window. She leaned back on her heels as if to twist around when faintly, from the edge of her windowsill, a little trill caught her attention.

Deirdre looked back to see Pahlah, the winged folisangel, balancing on the rooftop shingles. It strutted back and forth, making direct eye contact with her. Its wings waved rhythmically.

Deirdre tried to close the window. The winged cat had gotten her into a lot of trouble once already. As she reached for the window sash, however, Pahlah stopped. The creature faced her directly so the light from her bedroom would fall upon a note tied to its neck. Deirdre ushered the folisangel closer, and it obeyed.

After untying the black ribbon and note, Deirdre read the scrawled message: *Let Me In, Please.* This confused Deirdre for a moment because she didn't believe Pahlah could write, but the handwriting was atrociously messy. The folisangel crouched on its little hind legs and then leapt away from the window, flying off into the night.

"Strange," Deirdre mumbled to herself as she reached again for the window sash.

"Miss! Miss! Hello! Miss!" shouted a voice from the shadows in the street below.

Deirdre dropped her gaze first to the edge of the rooftop and then to the street beyond her front door. The hands of a boy were waving frantically.

"Miss! Hello! Did you read my note?" the boy shouted again; his whole body behaved spastically as if it were out of his control. He hopped to and fro in the street.

Without thinking, Deirdre leaned further out of her window. "Who are you?" she asked.

The boy was laughing wholeheartedly. "Please, I must speak with you," he managed to sputter before slipping into another fit of laughter.

"What's so funny?" Deirdre replied, befuddled by the fact that this boy, whom she had never met, had something to say to her. Perhaps it was a prank; a boy-joke.

"Nothing, it's just the muh-moonstone," the boy coughed.

Deirdre spotted a white glowing talisman on a silver chain around his neck. He was still jumping and laughing, but his jumps were, undoubtedly, growing in height. She watched the boy float up, up, up, and closer to her window. It was as if he were attached to a yo-yo string, being dropped and then tugged back up repeatedly.

"May I come in?" he asked while floating a short distance below her.

Deirdre stepped backward as the boy fell gently back towards the street before jumping one final time. He waved his hands around without any sense of control, but somehow, his feet landed on her windowsill. Ducking his head under the sash, he spread his arms and legs, pressing into the sides of the window frame.

He exhaled loudly, smacked his lips, and smiled. He seemed proud of himself and looked at her as if she should remark upon his impressive jumping.

Deirdre did not share in this feeling. She leaned against her bed and asked, "Who are you?" Her arms were folded firmly across her chest.

"Is that how you always greet people?"

Before Deirdre could form a proper reply, she noticed his moonstone flickering. Its glow faded back into the chunk of rock hanging from a silver chain. The boy also noticed this because his legs went all wobbly.

"Careful!" she exclaimed as he began to fall backward out of her window.

What happened next was a bit of a blur for both children. The boy let out a yelp, and Deirdre tugged at his shirt. Her momentum alone swung the stranger through her bedroom window. They both collapsed on the floor.

"Clever you!" the boy panted as he tugged at the pendant that hung around his neck, "and silly me." The silver chain snapped. He tossed the whole trinket to the side. Standing up as if nothing had happened, the boy brushed himself off and extended a dirt-glazed hand towards Deirdre. "Are you bumped?"

"No, I'm fine," Deirdre stammered. Her eyes thoroughly examined the boy for the first time. He was roughly her age, slim, and had a head of shaggy brown hair. His cheeks were decorated with freckles that emphasized his prominent dimples. "Are you Deirdre-Deirdre?" he asked directly.

Deirdre frowned, wondering why he had said her name in this way. Then she paused and stood to meet him at eye level. Cautiously, she nodded. "And who are you?"

"I'm James." Placing a hand on his stomach and the other behind his back, the boy then bowed low enough for his nose to float near his knee.

Although James was dressed in gray corduroys and a wrinkled white shirt splattered in mud, Deirdre recognized his formality and remembered her own. She curtsied before asking her unexpected guest, "What brought you to my window, James?"

"Three very important matters," he replied. "And the first is to attend your tea party."

-V-

FORGOTTEN MATTERS

James was an animated guest compared to the rest of Deirdre's High Sociotea members. His mannerisms, although fit for respectable company, were arguably a bit overzealous for just a gathering of two. But Deirdre didn't mind his flailing hands and darting gestures because they were well-accompanied by stories of James's grand adventures.

Deirdre imagined James and her father could be friends. Like Mr. Heart, James didn't fumble about with half-remembered facts while retelling his story. He offered acute interactions to ensure Deirdre was paying attention, and when the excitement rose in his voice, so did his ability to captivate her. Slowly the real world disappeared entirely, allowing Deirdre to walk within the landscapes of James's own words.

James's eyes were the distinct color of dark chocolate. Despite their inherent shade, they seemed to brighten more and more as he traveled from one story to the next. In truth, Deirdre became so charmed with his eyes and tales that she had completely forgotten to offer him a second cup of tea. That was until James released a rather inappropriate belch. He leaned back with a grin of contentment and said, "I'm talking too much. Tell me more about you, Miss Deirdre-Deirdre."

"It's just Deirdre," she corrected him.

"Just Deirdre," James repeated, his face wrinkled into confusion. When Deirdre nodded, he accepted the amendment and carried on by saying, "Well, Deer-Dra, tell me more about you. What adventures have you gone on?"

James waved his hand over his teacup and a small cloud of silver mist rose beneath it. The teacup hovered up to the bottom of his hand. "I don't come to Riverbed often. There aren't many adventures to be had around here, but Treliave lent me an eldestleaf and it brought me here…"

His voice carried on into another story, but Deirdre no longer paid attention. Her focus was on the floating cup. It had happened so instinctively for him, so naturally, as if this was an everyday occurrence. The teacup rolled over his fingers and then dropped down beneath his hand again — always being caught by the silver mist. Deirdre looked over the side of the table. There was no pollen pouch hanging from his belt. Squinting towards his fingertips, she didn't see a trace of silver pollen residue.

"… and then I made a deal with the wayfarers, and in return for giving you your mitten, I could then keep the —"

"Wayfarers?" Deirdre sputtered. "Mitten?"

"Yes." James stood abruptly. "Silly me, I almost forgot about the second important matter." He started patting down his pockets with the intent of producing a white mitten. "You left it in Marketfair."

Before Deirdre was willing to accept his word, she rushed over to her bed. Her hand reached the spot where she had hidden the lonely mitten before pulling it into view. "Does it match this one?"

While struggling to pat himself with one hand, James used his other one to point at the mitten. "Yep."

"That's my mitten!" Deirdre exclaimed.

"I know," James replied, confused by her declaration. His teacup began to wobble and float around him as a bumblebee might orbit a flower.

"How did you know it was mine?"

James passed it to her. "I told you. The Wayfarers entrusted me with the quest of bringing it to you in return for a treasure map." A look of excitement spread to the corners of his face as if this was the greatest trade he had ever made.

"A Wayfarer," Deirdre repeated worriedly.

James was notably less interested in the Wayfarer aspect of his story, and more inclined to talk about his treasure map. He nodded before catching his teacup and placing it back on the table. He waved away the silver cloud. "Her name was Vespra."

"I've met her," Deirdre said. A sense of dread began to creep up her spine, but then she caught sight of James's teacup wiggling on the edge of the table. "My cup!"

James shot out his hand towards the teacup despite being too far away to reach it, but the cup stopped falling and froze mid-drop.

"Oh, my quickness!" sighed James. "Don't worry. I got it." A fresh silver mist of pollen lifted the cup away from the floor.

But Deirdre was not worried; she was amazed. "You're really not from around here, are you?"

"Nope," James replied as he scooped up the cup and pressed it firmly onto the table. "I'm from the Tomadmann Gap, the southern opening to the River Olde." His matter-of-factness made Deirdre feel inferior. Mr. and Mrs. Heart had mentioned places beyond Bellebrook, but most of what she knew about maps had been taught to her in the Bellebrook schoolhouse. Her teacher had never mentioned anything about an "old river" or a "Madman gap." Deirdre thought about all the half-truths she had ever been told, more specifically about where eldestleaves came from. Her memory distinctly recalled the initial excitement in her mother's eyes when she had found one resting near the pine bridge. And then of course there was the very real possibility that one didn't need to use eldestree pollen to call. Perhaps Victriina had been right about calling with water. Deirdre felt a burning desire to ask James how he did it, but another question interrupted her.

"Do your parents know you've traveled this far?" she asked.

"Parents?"

"Yes, your parents," Deirdre restated. "I can't imagine what my parents would say if they knew I had left this house, let alone Bellebrook."

James sat down while he watched Deirdre place her mittens carefully on her nightstand. When she returned to the table, he said simply, "I can't imagine what my parents would say because I don't have any."

"You don't have parents?"

"None," James said with a sort of twisted smile.

"What about a grandparent or guardian?"

"I have Treliave. She raised me, but she doesn't make me stay with her. I stay and go as I want."

Deirdre offered James more tea, which he accepted.

"Treliave knows that I need to have adventures, that I need to have fun. I can't just sit around and host tea parties all day."

Deirdre did not take kindly to this snobbish remark. She assumed James wasn't a good enough host to receive such personal satisfaction from tea parties. "Sugar?" she asked him before sliding a small, lidded cup in his direction.

"Sugar in the shape of cubes?!" James shouted. "These are amazing!" Without caring to see Deirdre's reaction, James began examining a single square of sugar. He licked each side of the cube separately while giggling to himself.

A luminous white glow cast itself upon Deirdre's wall.

"Have you ever been to Auroval?" James asked. He brought the sugar cube so close to his face that his eyes went crossed. "This is a high-quality sugar box," he praised. "I've only had these twice in my life, and both times were when I stole a cup from a boring old friend. Everyone reads about adventures in Auroval. They don't actually like them the way I do."

Deirdre was nodding at his words but was intently staring at the white light continuing to grow up her wall. James's moonstone rose higher as he became more excited about the sugar cubes. "What's that, exactly?"

"Oh, mimble mumble!" James swore with a laugh. "That's a Moonstone Medallion."

"What's it for?"

"For floating, of course." James snatched the glowing medallion out of the air. He closed his eyes for a moment and began to smile. He giggled, and as he did his feet began to leave the floor. "Ta-Da!" he said as he reopened his eyes.

Deirdre gawked at him. "Children aren't allowed to use enchanted items or call pollen in Riverbed."

"I know." James sighed. "My friend Tasker can't do anything, but he's also too chicken to try."

"How did you learn? Is there a schoolhouse where you're from?"

"Nope. I taught me."

"But how?"

"By trying." James bumped his head on the ceiling. He pushed himself with his arms and flew over to the bed. Without pausing, he released the medallion and fell onto Deirdre's pillows.

"NO JUMPING ON BEDS!" screeched Mrs. Doris.

Deirdre leapt out of her seat. She had forgotten all about the grouchy old woman downstairs. She darted towards her bedroom door and replied, "Sorry, Mrs. Doris." The last thing Deirdre wanted was for her sitter to discover James floating around in her bedroom. A grunt of approval echoed its way up the stairs. Turning to face James, Deirdre put on her best hosting smile despite the onset of stress.

"Who's infecting the air with grump?" James asked.

"Grump?" Deirdre asked brightly in an attempt to distract James from the foulness below.

"It's like rotten cabbage," James explained while craning his neck to see the door behind her.

"Mrs. Doris is a rotten cabbage," Deirdre said absentmindedly as she ushered James back to his seat.

"Is she full of complaints?" James inquired. He wriggled around Deirdre as she tried to shove him in the opposite direction of her bedroom door.

"Yes. She's an old hag. A sour bag of bones."

"If she were a color, what color would she be?"

"Pea Green."

"Sounds like she has been infected with grump," James concluded.

Once Deirdre had smoothed out the wrinkles in her dress once more, she took her seat again at the table and stared at James. His eyes narrowed in focus at the door. Both of his arms were folded, and his once relatively good posture had gone slouch.

It was nearing Deirdre's bedtime, and she wasn't sure how late James intended to stay. She would have to ask him to leave eventually, but not knowing how, she stalled by politely asking, "What's the third very important matter?"

"The third?" James replied, more of a question for himself than for her. "The third matter is… tea… mitten…" He ticked off each matter by raising a finger. "Tea, mitten," James muttered with a frown. "I can't remember."

"Well," Deirdre prompted. "Retrace your steps."

"I've taken too many steps today. That would take forever."

"Don't actually retrace them," Deirdre said. "Just tell me about how you got here."

James nodded. "I woke up the other day and told Treliave I was leaving for an adventure. I wanted to go north, but she gave me an eldestleaf that brought me to Marketfair. I searched for adventures for a few days and eventually found the Wayfarers. I tried to steal their treasure map, but Vespra caught me. Instead of getting into trouble, she offered to make a trade for it. I had to return your mitten. Vespra told me you'd be hosting a tea party, and that I should attend it." James raised two fingers. "Tea and Mitten."

"What else did Vespra tell you?"

"That I should follow her folisangel to find you, but that isn't it." James looked towards Deirdre's window. "If I don't complete all three matters, I won't get that map." James pounded the table with his fist.

The teacups, saucers, and pot rattled. Deirdre was startled, and from below Mrs. Doris shouted. "Stop making noises this instant!"

"Grumpaguls," James whispered.

"Grumpa-whats?"

Strolling over to the edge of the room, James peered through the door. "It isn't just grump. There are Grumpaguls." Pulling the door wide open with an air of confidence, James marched out of the room. He was no longer interested in talk of tea and mittens. He was no longer interested in remembering his own third particularly important matter.

Deirdre tiptoed after James, hissing demands that he must return to her room at once, but it was useless. James was already hurrying down the stairs.

-VI-

NO TIME FOR QUESTIONS

"This is the last time I allow a stranger to attend my tea party," Deirdre promised herself as she crept out of her bedroom.

"James," she hissed.

Stepping onto the first-floor landing, James twisted around and answered quietly, "What?"

"Get back here. You're going to get me into trouble."

"But you're already in trouble! You're being held captive by Grumpaguls."

Deirdre made her hands into fists. She was sick of his nonsense. She had never heard of a Grumpagul before, and she was almost certain that "Grumpagul" was just a made-up word. "I don't care," she scowled. "Get back here!"

James raised a finger to his lips and looked towards Mrs. Doris.

"I hear footsteps," Mrs. Doris shouted without so much as turning around in her chair.

"Sorry," Deirdre replied as calmly as she could. James laid flat against the ground and began crawling along the floor.

Deirdre moved down the stairs to keep an eye on him, but with every step she took, the floorboards creaked.

"Why do I still hear footsteps?" Mrs. Doris sneered.

"I'm just going to feed my cat before he starts meowing. I don't want him to disturb you," Deirdre lied, at which point James had reached the threshold to the living room.

"What are you doing?" Deirdre mouthed silently at him.

"No time for questions," James responded while grinning mischievously. Then, leaning into Mrs. Doris's personal space, James positioned himself directly behind the old woman's left ear. Pinching his nose, he then pocketed all the air he could muster. When he could hold nothing else, he let it burst from his cheeks like a trumpet.

The burst of noise startled Mrs. Doris onto her feet. James squawked like a goose and raced into the room. He hopped onto the furniture to make himself as visible as possible. Deirdre could hear him laughing and hooting, pleased by Mrs. Doris's reaction.

"Children are not to be seen!" the old hag shrieked.

"But I'm see-able!" James countered. Bounding from one cushion to the next around the woman, he hollered, "Ca-Coo-Ca-Coo!"

Although terrified by the events unfolding, Deirdre couldn't stop herself from peeking around the corner and into the room. But what happened next made her wish she had stayed hidden up in her room.

The hunch-backed, bitter, old woman stood straight. Her exposed skin began to boil and pustulate. Mrs. Doris's voice fell to a more dangerous octave as she continued to holler after James.

"I command you to stop your nonsense at once!"

"But I'm having so much fun!"

"Children aren't meant to have fun," Mrs. Doris growled. Then her jaw unhinged. It hung open for a moment. Her tongue had turned black, and her teeth were coated in mucus that was the same color as her knitted scarf. From deep within her throat, a dark mass with amber eyes appeared. Mrs. Doris made a gurgling noise until a dark, oozing, slug-like creature flopped onto the floor. It smelled like spoiled milk.

"Not allowed to have fun?" James taunted. "Says who?" He continued antagonizing Mrs. Doris, visibly unsurprised by what had just happened.

"Don't talk back to me, wretched boy," Mrs. Doris snarled. Then more slug-monsters poured out of her mouth.

Her shadow became more menacing, growing beyond the framework of her own body and spreading like a storm.

"What are those?" Deirdre gasped.

"Grumpaguls, obviously," James said as he bounded around the room to be back by her side.

Mrs. Doris followed close behind. She was less cautious in her steps and squished a few of the slugs she had spewed.

"Come on," James said before giving Deirdre's arm a tug.

"You children will be punished!" Mrs. Doris declared as she stepped out into the hall. Her complexion had become sickly. The veins in her neck had turned purple, and the aged wrinkles in her skin dropped into longer, sagging folds. Deirdre was worried the woman was melting from the inside out.

"What do we do?" Deirdre asked as they backed away.

"Why are you asking me?" James replied though the gears in his mind were already spinning.

"You got me into this mess!"

"You were in this mess before I ever arrived. I've never seen so many grumpaguls in one lady," James said. "I want to count them."

Deirdre pulled James towards the kitchen. He produced a handful of sugar cubes and threw them into the growing army of slugs. As the frontline of grotesque creatures slurped over them, they shriveled, splattered, and then vanished.

"Keep doing that," Deirdre ordered, hurriedly climbing onto a chair so that she could reach the pot of hot soup her father had left on the stove.

"I'm all out," James said. "Those were the last ones. Silly me for not stealing more from you."

"Why were you stealing from me?" Deirdre snapped.

"No time for questions!" James said. He waved his hands like a music conductor towards the kitchen table and chairs. A silver cloud of pollen swirled around the furniture. James then pointed towards the entrance to the kitchen. The furniture floated across the floor like marionette puppets being yanked onto a stage. James piled them high to create a barricade between them and the grumpaguls.

"Don't break anything," Deirdre pleaded, fearing that her parents wouldn't believe that Mrs. Doris had vomited up monstrous slugs and attacked her. But then, she hoped perhaps her father might.

"It won't hold her for long," James warned.

A menacing scream sounded from the hallway. "I'll have you two hung by your toes!"

Suddenly a swarm of grumpaguls inched between the gaps of the barricade. Deirdre reached the hot soup she had failed to eat earlier and pulled on a pair of oven mitts. Carefully, she lifted the pot and aimed it towards the swarm. Then she tipped it.

Soup sloshed in a chunky cascade towards the slugs, but it did not affect them the same way as James's stolen sugar cubes. The grumpaguls snarled and swelled to the sizes of small dogs.

"You can't hurt a grumpagul with things that hurt!" James told her.

"Why didn't you tell me that!" Deirdre screamed in panic. She pressed herself against the cabinets as the grumpaguls slithered towards her.

"I thought you knew."

"Well, I didn't!"

James began ripping open all the cupboards and drawers while explaining, "Grumpaguls are rotten, bitter, spoil-spirited monsters. They feed on rude and grouchy people. Being aggressive and unkind only enhances their grumpiness. They don't like the sweet and delightful."

"Sweet and delightful?" Deirdre repeated from her corner of the kitchen. Other grumpaguls joined the oversized ones. Mrs. Doris had begun tearing down the barricade, continuously threatening them with different punishments. Terror overcame Deirdre. "We're trapped!"

"Not yet," James said with newfound excitement. He tossed a mixing bowl onto the counter. He pointed at different objects around the room. First, he called a bag of flour, then sugar, eggs, butter, and milk. He had Deirdre mix the ingredients while he scanned the open cabinets for sweet syrup and chocolate chips.

"James, why are we making cookies?" Deirdre asked.

"Sweet and delightful," he said before scooping some of the raw dough out with his bare hands. Taking aim, he then splatted the nearest grumpagul with the sugary treat. "What is more sweet and delightful than cookie dough?"

Deirdre was stunned by this improvised brilliance. Of course, she thought before adding extra chocolate chips to the bowl. Who could deny the delicious taste of double-chocolate chip cookies? Then she threw her own handful of cookie dough at the oncoming swarm of monsters.

"Look at this mess!" Mrs. Doris screamed as James kicked the half-emptied sugar bag onto the floor. "You wretched brats! You've ruined the floors. You've dirtied the counters. I'll have you —" But Deirdre never learned what Mrs. Doris was going to have her do because James had done something remarkable.

Flying off the counter with the mixing bowl in hand, James laid out in mid-air and poured the rest of the batter onto the old hag. It blinded, choked, and tripped her. She fell to the floor with a loud *crash*.

James dropped the empty bowl as he rolled across the floor. "I remember the third matter!" he hollered.

"What?" Deirdre asked. She stared at Mrs. Doris's limp figure as grumpaguls continued to crawl out of her mouth.

"The third matter!" James whooped. "I have unforgotten it. Come on!"

Deirdre and James dashed out of the kitchen and towards the stairs where a few straggling grumpaguls were waiting. Both James and Deirdre's hands were still covered in sticky sugar and chocolate, so it did not take much to defeat them. James squeezed a few like balloons until they popped, while Deirdre squished them like annoying flies.

"Why are we going back upstairs?" Deirdre asked as she followed James. "We should go out the front door."

"No time for front doors. No time for questions!"

"What will happen when my parents get home? What will they say when they see the mess we've made?" Suddenly, Deirdre was overcome by a new wave of dread. She skidded to a halt inside her room.

James leapt onto the bed and retrieved his moonstone medallion before answering, "We won't be here when that happens. We're running away."

"I can't just run away," Deirdre exclaimed.

James frowned. "But you must." He hopped off the bed. "Danger is here. We aren't safe."

"But, I —"

"No time!"

Deirdre wanted to continue arguing, but a part of her knew James was right. She could smell a renewed potency of sour milk wafting up the stairs. Her hands were not as sugary as before, so the fight back to the front door was impossible now. While hoping her parents would arrive, Deirdre grabbed her jacket, gloves, and windstone. She wanted to change out of her tea party dress but knew James would say there was no time.

"The third matter," James announced. "Is to hide under your bed." He lifted the bed skirt with a grin.

Deirdre didn't think. She listened without asking why. It seemed smart — hiding under a bed. If that was where monsters liked to hide when there were no lights on in the room, then non-monsters could reasonably do the same thing when the lights were on.

Scrambling under the bed as quickly as she could, Deirdre heard violent noises from the kitchen down below. Would she and James be able to hide here forever? Or for long enough for help to arrive? What would her parents say? What would Mrs. Doris and her grumpaguls do now?

Deirdre backed up into the shadows of her under-bed. There was no time for questions, or worries, or doubts, or fears. It seemed as if there was no time for anything now. This moment, Deirdre realized, was for beginning adventures that were beyond her control.

-VII-

THE ELDESTREE

"Watch it," Deirdre snapped as one of James's feet kicked her by accident.

"Sorry," he mumbled, wriggling the rest of the way beneath the bed. Their noses were filled with the smell of old wood floorboards and dust. Their shoulders touched. They both smelled of cookie dough. A monstrous shriek made them both shudder.

"Now what?"

James rolled onto his back and began examining the woodwork of the bed. "Ah-ha!" he said.

"What?"

"Clever me."

"What?" Deirdre watched as James traced his hand along the grooves of the bed frame. His finger stroked one of the discolored portions that had been chipped.

"Hold still and take my hand," James said shortly. He turned the palm of his right hand up so that she could grab it. "Close your eyes," he instructed while continuing to stroke the chipped part of the woodwork.

Hearing the heavy thumps of a disturbed Mrs. Doris startled Deirdre into obeying. She closed her eyes for only a moment to settle her fear. She was under her bed now. She was safe from the grumpaguls. Nothing could touch her or James except for a tiny little string that was tickling her nose.

"Treliave," James whispered.

The wooden floor turned soft, the air became crisp, and the crickets replaced the sounds of slugs being spewed across the floor.

"I am miraculous!" James cheered.

Deirdre opened her eyes and found herself lying belly-down on a soft patch of grass. A vine hanging from a nearby tree root replaced the bed frame above her. This root wasn't the kind Deirdre had been used to seeing. It was thick enough to support her whole family.

"We escaped back to Elderland!"

"Elderland?" exclaimed Deirdre as she fought her way out from beneath the root. Her father had mentioned this kingdom in his bedtime stories. Some of the most fantastic tales happened in this very place. But it was dark outside — as dark as it had been in Riverbed. The Crystal and Blood Moons were far off in the sky, casting a silvery red light along the dark grass and shadows.

James laughed heartily and hugged the tree root. "You're everywhere you need to be."

"I'm what?" Deirdre replied.

James leaned back and looked up, addressing the clouds. "Was this the adventure you promised? Because I didn't get the treasure map, well, not yet. I'll go back and get it." He paused to rub his chin. "Otherwise, it would be a foul trade."

"Map?" Deirdre questioned. "Who are you talking to?" She was tired of not having time for questions or answers.

Despite the warm jacket she wore, Deirdre was starting to shiver. Her eyes struggled to adjust to the night. But as she stepped away from the tree root, she began to realize that the tree it belonged to was no ordinary tree. She stepped back, no longer attentive to James's lunacy. Her gaze was held at the top of the vast canopy of leaves — leaves that, even in the dark, were visibly massive. The trunk would easily occupy an entire block in Bellebrook.

Something crunched beneath Deirdre's foot. It felt like a thin branch. She glanced down and gasped, looking closer. It was a stem to a leaf. "This… this is an eldestleaf!"

"Obviously," James replied.

And then Deirdre realized exactly where she was. Her hand instinctively felt for her windstone. "This is Treliave, the eldestree. My father told me a story about her. I saw one of her leaves by Marketfair!" Deirdre stared at the yellow leaf. Had she laid herself on it, she would have the same rolling-about space as she had on her bed. "Where is my bed?" Deirdre asked.

James shrugged and gestured towards the eldestree. "You'll have to ask her."

"Should I introduce myself?" Deirdre asked while looking up at the tree. Nothing happened. Treliave remained in her tree-ish state.

James, however, received some sort of answer because he answered by saying, "Treliave says you look cold, and you're welcome to come up into the treehouse if you'd like."

"A treehouse?"

James nodded. He climbed onto one of the roots and walked cat-like over towards the trunk. Then he placed his right hand over his heart and his left hand on the eldestree. "Look up," he said to Deirdre.

Deirdre did as instructed. Up in the heart of the canopy, she saw golden light drip out of the eldestree's trunk. A little cottage embedded within the heart of the tree revealed itself to her. It had three porches, a dozen windows, arched doorways perched over different branches, and a chimney. Fluorescent mushrooms the size of stepping-stones began to grow from the base of the tree — positioning themselves in the form of a staircase. Deirdre's mouth hung agape in amazement as the mushrooms sprouted higher and higher, spiraling up and around Treliave before ending at the lowest porch of the treehouse.

"Coming?" James asked.

Deirdre could only nod happily in response. Despite the dim

moonlight, she slowly turned in a circle, eyes trained upwards, trying to capture all the details of the eldestree. Eventually, she felt James take her hand. He helped her scramble up to the root he was standing on, which led them easily to the mushroom staircase. A slightly sticky residue coated the top of each step.

The climb was tiresome, but Deirdre wondered if it was because the excitement had become a calmer kind of excitement. There was no danger here. She also considered her relative weariness could be attributed to the fact that it was well past her bedtime. Thoughts about the soup that was spilled across the kitchen floor struck Deirdre. She cringed but quickly told herself there was no time right now to fret. She was too far away from it all to do anything.

Warm, flickering light peeped out of the many windows. Little intertwining branches formed a porch railing. Every detail about the cottage seemed to be made from a part of the eldestree. The roof that sloped over the porch was made from eldestleaves. The door ahead of Deirdre was fashioned from thick chunks of bark. The whole structure reminded Deirdre of the birdhouses she sometimes made with her mother, but naturally, this house was much larger.

"Treliave prefers shoes on the porch," James informed Deirdre as they stepped off the final mushroom.

Deirdre followed his instructions silently. She was still busy taking in her surroundings. The branches of the eldestree looked like roadways and bridges as they twisted and stretched over themselves. With the new vantage point, Crystal moonlight now reached the trunk and various arms of the tree. Deirdre looked through the large leaves and saw a great expanse of stars.

James opened the front door. Walking in ahead of her, James stretched out his arms as wide as he could. He let out a dramatic yawn and spun around to see Deirdre's reaction.

"This is amazing!" she said, following him inside. The door calmly closed itself behind her. Warmth seeped into her toes and chilled cheeks. High ceilings arched over her in organic undulations. It was one beautiful trunk of lightwood hollowed out into a cozy dwelling with four alcoves, three different sets of stairs, and a den, complete with a fireplace.

Deirdre examined the hearth. It was shaped like the one in her own house, but the wood wasn't burning in it. Instead, Deirdre saw a golden bowl with shimmering liquid set ablaze.

She moved over to a set of high shelves. They held a collection of mismatched items; a glass scale for pricing pollen, an ordinary-looking lump of coal, a stack of iron coins, and an ivory box with golden clasps. Next to it was a dull-looking set of tin mugs, a mason jar labeled "Bursts of Glee," and a set of green and golden rings.

James appeared beside Deirdre and placed his moonstone medallion beside a white stick.

"Yup, all of these things are mine," he bragged. Then he slid his hands into the pockets of his mud-stained pants. "Most were found on my adventures."

"What adventure is this one from?" Deirdre asked, pointing towards the lump of coal.

"The Wyldar Woods."

Deirdre raised an eyebrow.

"It's located in Riverbed. How have you not heard of the Wyldar?" James paused in disbelief. "The Undead Wood, Woodland Black, the Poison Sap Ring?" He listed each name as Deirdre continued shaking her head. "What about the Wylde Woods? It surrounds the Wyldar."

"I've heard of Farwood," Deirdre said, trying to sound more knowledgeable.

James waved her comment away like a foul stench. "The Farwood is boring, but this…" He held up the chunk of coal. "This is dirt from the Wyldar Woods." He whispered the name cautiously and then placed the coal back delicately.

"So, it's dirt?"

"Dirt from one of the most dangerous places in the world. Dirt from a forest so scary and so evil that very few who enter it come back alive."

Deirdre frowned in disbelief. "You've been there?"

"I have," James said.

Pointing towards the ivory box, Deirdre asked, "What's in there?"

"Nothing."

"Nothing?"

James looked at it but left it on the shelf. "Treliave told me it would open when I had something worthy of putting inside it."

"So, it's an enchanted box?"

"Yup. It's what started my collection."

"Where did you get it?"

"I've always had it. Treliave said it was a gift along with the white stick, but she never tells me who gave it to me." James's stomach growled. "Are you hungry?" he asked Deirdre.

Starving was the word Deirdre would have used to describe herself, but she had been taught that it was rude to express one's own hunger in front of strangers. She followed James to a large table. He promptly set two plates on either end. They were gold like the bowl in the hearth. From there, James moved over towards a wall where honeycomb-shaped holes dripped water into a decanter. He brought it over to the table and poured some of the liquid onto his plate.

"I'd like apple pie, please," he said. The water sizzled and hissed until — poof — a personal apple pie appeared on his plate. "What would you like?" James asked.

Deirdre was dumbfounded. Her parents had used pollen for many things, but never to create a meal out of water. Then again, she wasn't quite sure it was pollen that had turned the water into a pie. The smell from James's plate encouraged her answer. "Apple pie," she said.

"No, no," he corrected her and refrained from pouring water onto her plate. "You must say apple pie, please."

"I'd like apple pie, please," Deirdre said out loud.

James poured water on the plate. It sizzled and hissed until — poof — another personal apple pie appeared. "Dig in," he told her.

Both children had three servings worth of food. James had an apple pie, peach cobbler, and broccoli. Deirdre, feeling guilty about having dessert before her supper, had a serving of tomato soup followed by corn mixed in mashed potatoes. James helped himself to a spoonful of Deirdre's potatoes without asking, and Treliave scolded him for it. Deirdre hadn't heard the tree, but a vine grew from the ceiling and flicked James's wrist as if warning him not to behave so poorly.

When they were done eating, James led Deirdre with her dirty plate to a separate basin of water. It flowed like a little river from left to right around the edge of a wall. There was a chunk of moss and a towel beside it. James washed his plate first to show her the process. Deirdre was secretly relieved that he had. Her parents had never taught her. Surely, she could have figured it out, but James's guidance gave her the confidence to learn and do it on her own.

Afterward, James led Deirdre to a room on the right side of the treehouse. "You can sleep here tonight," he told her as they approached a doorway. "Treliave can prepare a room for you." James placed his right hand against his heart and his left upon the door. "A bedroom for Deirdre, please."

A moment later, a wooden knob appeared beneath James's hand. He gave it a twist and pushed the door open. Inside, Deirdre found a bed frame identical to the one in her room. There were blankets and pillows, and a glass goblet holding liquid fire.

"What's that?" Deirdre asked, noticing a thin line of silver light flowing from the floor to the ceiling.

"That," James answered, "is an eldestree vein." He rolled back his sleeve to reveal his forearm. Deirdre looked at her own to see blue veins beneath her skin. "That's where pollen is stored."

"How do people get pollen from there?"

"Like any normal tree, Treliave sheds her pollen in the spring. Riverbed people and Wayfarers camp out around her and collect what she gives for the year." James paused. "Treliave says you look tired and that I should let you sleep."

"What about my parents?" Deirdre asked. She didn't want her mother and father to worry about her all night.

Not knowing how to respond, James looked up at the ceiling. "Treliave says you should rest and leave such worries for later."

"Later?"

James nodded.

Deirdre looked up at the ceiling, hoping to see words or hear the eldestree as James did. "Why can't I hear what she says?"

"I don't know."

"Well, ask her."

James did so, though he was not happy about being bossed around in his own treehouse. After a moment he shrugged. "She isn't replying."

"Does she do that often?"

"Only when she can't answer a question. There are laws and things," James said with a yawn. He walked towards the door as if this settled the matter.

Deirdre was not content with this response. She was accustomed to being told half-truths when questions could not be given answers. Never had Deirdre been completely ignored.

And yet, with her eyes heavy, belly full, and mind exhausted, she accepted defeat. James left for his own room elsewhere. Deirdre closed the door gently and proceeded to look around. There was a little mirror hanging on the wall above a small bathing sink. Her reflection revealed she had cookie dough smeared on her forehead and cheeks. The same honeycomb spout Deirdre had seen earlier trickled freshwater into the room. She washed the dough off as best as she could.

On the furthest side of the room, there was a window and a door. It led out onto one of the porches Deirdre had seen while climbing up to the treehouse. Too tired to investigate it, Deirdre removed her jacket and hung it on a bottom bedpost. She felt both pockets to ensure her mittens were safe inside and then removed her windstone.

The thought of sending the stone to her parents at that moment crossed her mind, but the fact that she also had it made her feel safe. A piece of her parents was with her so long as she kept it. Deirdre figured that Treliave would look after her and get her home safely in the morning. She placed the windstone on a nightstand. White moonlight slipped through the trees and through the window with ease. Deirdre ruffled the blankets as she climbed into bed. She blew on the flame in the goblet, but to her surprise, it didn't extinguish. Liquid fire and liquid food, she thought. "I'd like no light, please," she said out loud. The flame in the goblet fizzled out. All that remained was the silver vein and the windstone, which was glowing a soft white.

-VIII-

THE ADVENTURE MAP

Deirdre rose the following morning with the belief that she had just had the best sleep of her life — and she was right to believe so. Sleeping in the heart of an eldestree has many benefits. The leaves operate like dreamcatchers, trapping the wandering thoughts of the world before they can enter resting minds. The bark of an eldestree is thick and perfect for blocking out the sounds of disrespectful bugs and birds that buzz and tweet before the sun even rises. And the tree itself, of course, emits a hum that is both too soft for humans to hear and yet just strong enough for them to feel. The vibrations run up and down the whole of the tree, from its base to its branches; a gentle hum passing through the hollowed areas, amplified for the most careful listeners to hear...

...and perhaps Deirdre would have heard it had James not started making a ruckus out in the main room. Deirdre rubbed the last sights of her dream away and blinked. Instinctively, her hands patted the mattress with the expectation of finding Mr. Button, but he wasn't there. The next step in Deirdre's typical morning would have been to look for him, but the windstone caught her attention. Sunlight was streaming onto it now; the stone sparkled like a diamond with a thousand edges.

Memories of the night rushed in as Deirdre looked around the room. She saw her jacket hanging from the bedpost. The walls of the eldestree were bare but not bland. Their organic lines and grooves ran around the room as one unified image.

Deirdre's eyes went from the jacket to the blankets she had cocooned herself in, then back to the windstone. Something flew by the window. Its shadow cut across the bedspread; its shadow was too big to belong to a bird. But Deirdre wasn't quick enough to see what it was. Then more banging echoed from the main room.

"Mimble mumble!" James swore. "Sticky spoiled sour slime!" More clattering and crashing followed.

Curious about the commotion, Deirdre hopped out of bed. She took the Windstone and placed it back in her coat pocket. The floor was warm beneath her feet. It took a moment, when Deirdre wrapped her fingers around the door handle, to have the courage to open it. She hadn't brought a change of clothes. Her dress, which had been presentable yesterday, was now wrinkled from being used as a nightgown. Her blonde hair, which was always brushed before breakfast, was now disheveled and knotted. Nothing could be done to it. However, this didn't stop her from quickly running her fingers through it.

"Tangled thistle thorns!" James shouted.

"What's wrong?" Deirdre inquired as she stepped out of her room. To her relief, she saw that James was still wearing his mud-stained pants, and although he had changed his shirt, it was arguably more wrinkled.

"It has a hole." James lifted up a sock.

Deirdre giggled at the pure dismay in James's furrowed brow. "You're throwing a tantrum over a sock?"

"It has a hole," he repeated with emphasis on the final word. "Why are you laughing?"

"I'm not."

"You are."

Deirdre couldn't help herself. Although James had heard Deirdre, he had not stopped staring at the dirty sock dangling between his pinched fingers. It had grass stains and blue smears all over it. It had clearly spent several days beneath his bed.

"I could sew it for you," Deirdre offered.

"No thread," James said while bringing the sock as close to his face as possible. "No needle."

"Don't you have another pair of socks?"

James whispered insults to his sock. "They aren't as comfy as this pair," he finally said.

"Couldn't you use pollen to fix it? Do you need some special words?" Deirdre thought about the phrase used to start her tea parties.

James paced back and forth across the main room. One bare foot stomped alongside a socked one. "No. That won't work," he said. "I'll have to get a new pair." Throwing the sock with a hole out of sight, he then turned to address Deirdre more directly. His chipper demeanor returned. "Good morning," he said.

"Good morning."

"Would you like some breakfast?" James asked. He then pointed towards the table where he had, at some point earlier that morning, set up a tray with fruit and biscuits.

Deirdre nodded with a bright smile. This was an overly sweet gesture. When she saw the fruit, however, she raised an eyebrow at it. "What's that?"

"An eldaple."

"Is it like an apple?"

James scooped one from the tray, rubbed it against his arm for a good polish, and presented it to her. "It's like an apple," he said. "But it has wedges on the inside, and you have to peel the skin. Oh, and there are seeds which you can eat, but you need to spit the shells."

Deirdre took the ruby-red fruit into her hand. It weighed and felt like an apple. It did not strike her as smushable. What was most odd to her, however, was how perfectly round it was.

Despite seeing James chomping away at one, Deirdre felt unsure about eating something that resembled the likes of a juggling ball. She put hers back on the table and reached for a biscuit instead.

"So, what adventure are we going on today?" James asked. He spat a shell onto the floor.

"Adventure? I need to go home."

"Go home?"

"Yes," Deirdre said firmly. "My parents will be worried sick."

James frowned. Parents were always getting in the way of him sharing adventures with other kids his age. "Can't you go home tomorrow?" he pouted. "Today has the best weather for adventuring." He grabbed another eldaple, dug his nails into the skin, and peeled it away in segments. "Treliave agrees with me."

Deirdre didn't believe him. "Take me home and maybe we can go on an adventure tomorrow."

"It will take forever to get you home." James sighed. "Can we at least have an adventure on the way to Riverbed?"

"Forever is an awfully long time."

"At least a day."

"A day?"

"We have to go towards Auroval before we can go back to Riverbed."

Deirdre felt puzzled. "We have to go east in order to go west?" James bobbed his head as if this were common logic. "Can't you just use pollen to take me back?"

"How would I do that?"

"You've already done it!" Deirdre exclaimed. "Last night, under my bed."

James chuckled as he popped a wedge of fruit into his mouth. He walked around the table towards one of the empty walls in the main room. "I didn't use pollen for that. There was an enchantment already in the bed. I just had to call for Treliave."

"There was an enchantment on my bed?"

"You didn't know?"

Deirdre shook her head. "Children in Riverbed aren't allowed to use enchantments or pollen."

"Maybe your parents put it there," James said.

Deirdre didn't fully believe him. Had they placed something as important as an enchantment on her bed, wouldn't they have told her? And even if they hadn't, why would their enchantment take her to an eldestree? "Do you know my parents?" Deirdre asked Treliave. She looked to James for a reply.

Whether Treliave answered her or not, James didn't say. He seemed distracted by the empty wall in the main room.

Deirdre walked over to where he stood and realized that the natural lines of the eldestree were vanishing. In its place were harder, darker lines. They bent and curved purposefully until a large map of the continent was completed. Small words detailed the different towns of Riverbed and Elderland. A long waterway entered from the south beside Treliave and severed the eastern lands from Riverbed. The waterway was called the River Olde, and it bent its way eastward towards Auroval. Deirdre naturally looked towards home. She saw towns like Mill Pond, Blaemede, Merrivyne, and her own Bellebrook. There was even a small dot to mark the campgrounds of Marketfair.

"It's my Adventure Map," James told her. "It only shows where I've been."

The lines continued to fill in parts of Farwood, the long edges of the Wylde Woods in the north, and lastly, a small black blotch labeled the Wyldar Woods. Deirdre didn't say anything, but that didn't stop James from muttering a satisfactory, "I told you so."

When the map finally completed all of its details, James approached it with a familiar eye. He raised an index finger. "This is the River Olde," he told Deirdre while tracing it. "The water is too fast to cross where we are, but if we follow it this way," he said as he traced it east, "the water becomes swimmable near Mill Pond."

Deirdre turned pink with embarrassment. "I don't know how to swim," she stammered.

James looked away from the map, blinked as if to process her words, and then turned back to the map. "So, we'll swim across the River Olde here and end up near Mill Pond. My friend Tasker can find us a vegetable cart that is traveling to Marketfair. We can take that down the Great Road and then walk to your house from there. You know how to get to your house, right?" James remembered he had followed Pahlah all the way to her window.

"I don't know how to swim," Deirdre repeated sheepishly.

"So?" James answered. "Adventures are for learning." A section of Mill Pond grew bold for a moment, with a place labeled the Harvesting Hills.

Deirdre noticed that James hadn't seen it. "Harvesting Hills?" she inquired.

James was rummaging through the bowl of fruit as he replied, "What about it?" Then his fingers curled around another eldaple.

"What is it?"

"Why?"

"It's on the map."

Rather than looking at the map, James looked at the ceiling. Drawn above him, in the same thick lines, was a moon chart. The three moons were each depicted; the Frostforth moon was colored a bright blue, the Crystal moon was cloudy white, and the Blood moon was a deep red. All three moons were positioned around a large ring, which was used to see where the moons were in their seasonal rotation. The brightest moon was the Crystal moon. It took possession of the night sky during both spring and autumn. In the chart, it was positioned on the ring.

Deirdre followed James's gaze. Moon charts were an important study in school. Deirdre could see the blue moon was glowing the second brightest within the ring. It was the next moon to rise, and upon its arrival, the season of frostforth would begin. The Blood moon, dimmest and drawn outside of the rotation ring, was the moon of heatspell. Its possession of the night was coming to an end.

"Splendid," James whispered with a mischievous grin. His eyes glanced back at the map and then at Deirdre. "Well, if you want to get home there's no time to waste."

"I'll get my coat," Deirdre replied. She hurried back up to the room in which she had slept. James snuck a glance up at Treliave with the same grin as before.

Deirdre returned to the main room with her coat on and mittens in hand. She found James by the dining table preparing a bundle. He filled it with leftover biscuits, bursts of glee, and a few more eldaples. He secured it all to a stick that Treliave offered him.

"Ready?" Deirdre asked. Conflicting feelings abruptly knocked together in her stomach. A part of her was excited to go home, and another was afraid. Though her time spent in the eldestree had been short, something about leaving it felt strangely wrong. The last time Deirdre had felt this way, her mother had taken her to one of the flower gardens in Bellebrook. It had been a beautiful afternoon, with vibrant petals of dazzling, ever-changing colors. Deirdre had enjoyed every moment of it, but when her mother said it was time to go, Deirdre felt this same sense of helplessness. That night, a strong storm passed through the town with heavy rain and strong winds. All the petals were torn free from their stems. Now, in the heart of the eldestree, Deirdre worried about what would happen.

James skipped about the room. "I'm not ready yet," he said before walking back to his adventure map. The wall was blank again, but this didn't seem to bother him. He rotated his free hand and placed his palm against the wall.

Deirdre regarded these motions with silent curiosity.

A thick silver line rose beneath the tip of James's thumb. It darted around the surface of the wall and made an outline of a sword. Bits of wood began to splinter and chip. Dust settled on James's feet while the eldestree wall rumbled. The sword slowly gained shadow and depth as it lifted off the surface of the wall and into James's hand. In the end, his finger curled around the formed hilt and he pulled the sword free.

"Now I'm ready!" James declared, swinging a newly fashioned wood sword around.

-IX-

SAILING DOWN THE RIVER OLDE

The moment James slid the wooden sword between his belt and pants, Deirdre yearned for one herself. Never in her life had she seen a real sword. The sensible part of her wondered if wooden swords counted. Regardless, Deirdre felt worthy of any sword after squishing grumpaguls with her bare hands, wooden sword or otherwise. To her mild disgruntlement, James did not offer to get her one, and Treliave gave no indication to Deirdre on how to pull a sword free from the wall.

Mr. Heart told Deirdre wonderful bedtime stories about mysterious swords. Her favorite was about an invisible blade called the Sword of Atloria. It was said that when the blacksmith first crafted it, he found he could not bear to make a blade for the jewel-encrusted hilt. Instead, the unfinished sword was gifted to the princess of Atloria as a request to maintain peace and order in the Kingdom. The day came, however, when pirates laid siege from the sky. The princess raced to her room and grabbed the unfinished sword with the intention of only hiding it. But at that moment she discovered a blade of white-hot light bloomed from the hilt. The blade cut through steel as if it were a stick of butter.

With swift feet and nimble actions, the princess fought off the pirates single-handedly. When the city was safe once more, the blade of the sword vanished. Only in times of danger did it ever reappear — or so Deirdre's father claimed.

Deirdre would have shared this story with James, but he was already rushing ahead, ready to begin the adventure to Bellebrook. She followed him silently to the porch where they had left their shoes. Deirdre peered over the guardrail, expecting to see the mushroom staircase, but there wasn't one. She gulped down her nerves, hoping that the eldestree was not expecting them to climb down on their own.

Deirdre kept her gaze forward and looked out through the branches. All the trees were dressed in their autumn best. Far-off fields were growing pumpkins that looked no bigger than insects from where Deirdre stood. Even further west on the horizon she saw smoke curling into the sky; she reasoned it must be from an exceptionally large chimney.

"Let's go, let's go," James ordered enthusiastically, gripping Deirdre's wrist and pulling her back into the treehouse.

Leading her to the fireplace, James snatched the large golden bowl and moved it out of his way. He crouched down and knocked on the back wall of the fireplace three times. "A way out, please," he said.

At this point, Deirdre knew better than to expect nothing. The wall slid to the side and James smiled. He passed Deirdre their knapsack.

"You carry it," he told her.

"Why?"

"Because I need to hold onto this," James explained impatiently. He drew his sword while seating himself in the fireplace, his legs resting in the tunnel that had appeared.

"Can't I hold the sword?" Deirdre asked hopefully.

James scooted forward. "No," he said. Then he scooted further into the tunnel and vanished.

Deirdre knew she would have to follow James, but she could not suppress her desire to have a sword of her own. Resting the knapsack by the fireplace, Deirdre ran over to the Adventure Map. The outline for James's sword had healed; smooth bark had grown over the distinctive mold. Deirdre stuck out her hand as James had done, inhaled a great breath, and waited.

At first Deirdre was filled with patience. Her posture was beautifully straight. Her eyes remained shut. She waited a whole minute before she felt as though it wasn't working. Removing her hand from the wall, she rubbed it on her dress. Perhaps it was too dirty, she thought.

With a touch more assertiveness, Deirdre placed her hand back on the wall. She waited again, but with a little less patience, Deirdre waited a whole thirty seconds before looking at Treliave.

"May I please have a sword too?" she asked.

Treliave didn't respond.

"Why did he get one?"

Treliave didn't respond.

Deirdre removed her hand. She stepped back sadly and was about to turn away when lines began to appear. They zigzagged and scribbled wildly along the whole length of the wall. A detailed map of the Tomadmann Gap, the River Olde, Mill Pond, and the Harvesting Hills were quickly labeled. A silver line decorated with tiny footprints forged a path, illustrating where Deirdre and James were supposed to go. As the line snaked away, Wylde and Wyldar Woods appeared.

As the footprints approached the small position of the Wyldar Woods discovered by James, more woods were drawn in. The line traveled deeper into the forest. A mountain appeared without a label, and an ambiguous "X" marked the spot.

"We're going to Bellebrook," Deirdre told Treliave. "I have to go home."

The "X" shined brighter.

"My parents are waiting for me."

The image of the map rapidly sunk into the bark. Deirdre began to back away, wondering if she had angered the eldestree. As she did, however, a new image appeared in thick cursive words:

Truth Will Find You Soon. The Black Star Will Fall.

Deirdre shuddered. She remembered those words belonging to the Wayfarer, Vespra. Her right heel bumped into one of the dining chairs. She stumbled. Averting her eyes away from the words, Deirdre rushed towards the fireplace. She scooped up the knapsack and crawled into the tunnel. The floor beneath her turned slick and sloped.

Deirdre slipped. She dropped the knapsack as she curled into a ball. The last thing she saw was the stick whooshing away ahead of her as she spiraled around a bend. The light from the treehouse vanished.

Down, down, down Deirdre went, gathering speed and feeling the air rush past her ears. Every couple of feet she slid past little pieces of neon-purple glowing fungus. They didn't illuminate the tunnel as much as they outlined the path she was zooming down. Deirdre's worries shifted as daylight suddenly broke through the darkness of the tunnel. The slick wooden surface abruptly changed to wet grass. Deirdre rolled and tumbled to a stop.

"Good thinking," James hollered. "If you hadn't sent the knapsack first, we'd have been bumped all over."

Deirdre straightened up and glanced around. She spotted James standing on the edge of a cliff. "What?" she replied. Thoughts of Truths and Stars plagued her mind.

"You were taking too long, so I started climbing up the tunnel to see if you got stuck. Then the knapsack went sliding past me and I figured you'd be right behind it. I slid down double fast to avoid a bad bumping."

Deirdre didn't say anything back. Her eyes were busy examining the fresh grass stains rubbed into her wrinkled dress. She frowned.

A warm breeze ruffled her hair. The air was heavy with salt and mist. Deirdre looked towards the cliffside again, intent on discovering more about her surroundings. It had been so dark when she and James had arrived beneath the eldestree.

Deirdre turned around. She noted that the tunnel she had just tumbled from was beginning to heal over with fresh bark, just like the wall from which James had pulled his sword free. Deirdre followed the trunk of the tree up and fell into instant awe. The eldestree reached higher than she had realized. It was as if it existed as a bridge between the land and sky. Even after tilting her head all the way back, Deirdre could not even glimpse the top branches. Her sky was made up of red, orange, and gold leaves.

James waited a moment with an easy smile on his face. He had known Treliave his entire life, but it never stopped him from feeling humbled by her incomparable greatness.

Deirdre reached up to touch a root, then she turned to see more roots lifting and diving out of the ground. Their thickness was impressive; they alone could have been mistaken for fallen trees. She ran her hand along the length of one to the cliffside where James stood. Deirdre smelled the breath of the sea again. "Is that —"

"Aramayus Bay," James confirmed.

Behind him and over the side of the cliff was a vast turquoise surface of water. Deirdre had seen it once before. She watched the waves lap against the shore, and the bright blue water swayed out into the beyond. It was more magnificent than she remembered. Standing between this and the eldestree made her feel ridiculously small.

She pointed towards a gap in the land. A narrowing waterway rushed deep into a valley of rolling hills and young trees. "That's the Tomadmann Gap!" she said.

"Yep. The start of the River Olde. We should start following it," James said. He turned on the spot with his chest held high. His next adventure was about to begin.

Leading Deirdre along another root system, they walked down the back of the hillside, following a narrow foot-trodden path that led away from the Aramayus. It gradually began to run parallel to the River Olde. There was no clear transition between the sounds of waves crashing against the cliffside and the rowdy rampant rapids of the river. White foam hissed and sloshed against clusters of smoothed boulders.

Although they were far from Treliave's trunk, her shade still reached over their path. Deirdre couldn't help but look in every direction with unblinking eyes. Bellebrook and the surrounding landscapes of Riverbed were beautiful and quaint. She had always felt at home in the gardens and cobblestone roads. Here, however, Deirdre felt infinite excitement. She unexpectedly understood James as she watched him trot ahead with his wooden sword in hand. There was so much more of this world to see. How could she spend so much time in Riverbed?

"This is the spot," James confirmed.

"The spot to what?"

James rolled his eyes and sheathed his sword. He pulled back his shoulders to add importance to what he had to say. "The spot where Sea Monsters can't swim."

Deirdre's neck whipped to the River Olde; her eyes boggled. "Sea Monsters?"

"Sea Monsters," James repeated.

"So, we follow the River from here?"

"No."

Deirdre raised an eyebrow. "No?"

James nodded to confirm. "From here we shall sail."

"Sail on what?"

"An eldestleaf, of course."

"Because the monsters can't swim this far."

"Exactly," James answered with a twisted smile. "No slimy, scaled, slithering saber-toothed, swimming snakes are going to catch us from way down here!" He shook a triumphant fist towards the Aramayus as if some sea monsters had been listening.

Deirdre looked back towards Treliave. A gust of wind rolled across her branches and gently tugged at the maple-shaped leaves until one sprang loose. The wind instantly settled itself. Everything became still.

A shadow twirled on the ground in front of them, growing bigger as the freed leaf above fell. Not wanting to be crushed by it, Deirdre jumped back. The leaf came to rest gently on the edge of the water between her and James.

"Did you know that would happen?" Deirdre asked when she noticed James was smiling.

"Treliave suggested it when you said you couldn't swim. She knew we needed to travel down the river, so she gave us a way." James waved at Treliave in thanks.

Deirdre followed suit, even though it felt a bit strange. The trees in her own backyard were not this smart or generous, but Deirdre quickly doubted this assumption. Perhaps the trees in Bellebrook were just as intelligent. Deirdre made a mental note to investigate further upon her return home.

James leaned against the stem of the eldestleaf. He pushed it with all his might. His face turned bright red as he heaved his weight into it, but their newly fashioned boat would not budge. Looking puzzled, James stepped back to roll up his sleeves. His jaw tightened, but a moment later he was back at it — shoving the leaf towards the River Olde with all of his strength and with no success.

"Oh, mimble mumble," he swore.

"Do you need a hand?" Deirdre asked.

"No," James returned quickly. "I can do it." Again and again, he tried, pushing against different parts of the leaf. This had not been the first eldestleaf he had sailed on. James had floated along the River Olde plenty of times before, and every time he had, the leaf scooted into the water with ease. "Don't be so stiff," he snapped at the leaf.

"Let me try," Deirdre suggested.

"I can do it," James snapped.

Frowning at his stubbornness, Deirdre placed the knapsack on the ground and nudged James aside. "Well, it doesn't look like you can," she told him. Positioning herself against the stem as James had done, Deirdre then pushed. Her efforts also proved to be useless. "Can't you use polled to make it move?"

"Nah," James sighed. "It's no good when it comes to Treliave."

"Well, then let's try pushing it together," Deirdre said. She wasn't going to let something as silly as a heavy leaf stop her from getting home. James came to Deirdre's side with a nod.

"On the count of three," he said. "One, two, three!"

They both shoved the eldestleaf with all the power they could muster. Their combined force proved to be not only enough but too much. Both tumbled over their own feet and incidentally rolled onto the top of the leaf. There was a boisterous splash as the boat bobbled into the river. Luckily neither of them got terribly wet.

The scarlet leaf bounced up and down several times as the waves of the Aramayus took hold. Deirdre and James saw one another's dazed faces and laughed in triumph as they sat up to see the shrinking shoreline. A look of terror fell over James's face. "Drats," he said.

"What is it?" Deirdre asked.

James pointed back towards the grass where Deirdre had set down the knapsack. "Our snacks," he groaned.

"We can go back," Deirdre said.

"Can't," James replied flatly. "The current is too strong. We won't be able to drift towards shore until we make it around Big Bend."

"How far is that?"

James shrugged. "Too far for us to turn back."

Deirdre grimaced and crossed her legs. She hated feeling as if it was her fault, but James didn't say anything more on the subject. Deirdre pretended to be distracted by the water running beneath them. She rested her chin in the palms of her hands while staring downstream.

"How far until the Big Bend?"

"No going back," James said groggily. Closing his eyes and lying down on his portion of the leaf, he added, "It's part of the adventure now."

"But what if we go hungry? How will we eat?" Deirdre worried.

James didn't reply.

For a moment she watched him, afraid of what might happen if the leaf capsized or suddenly started to sink. Part of her wanted to shake him awake; this was not an appropriate time to sleep. But the rhythmic lull of the River Olde calmed her, as did the light which sparkled off its surface. On the soft edges of the current, she noticed little fish with rainbow scales. She saw purple-spotted frogs with yellow beaks on the riverbanks. Overhead, flocks of birds seemed to lead the way from above.

It seemed strange to her that such exotic creatures could live just across the shores of the River Olde. Why didn't they migrate into Riverbed? Deirdre thought about Pahlah and how until that moment, she had never encountered a folisangel. Were there more winged cats camping and flying over the meadows in Elderland? Deirdre kept an active watch, hoping to glimpse one in the passing fields.

New trills and chirps came from the long-grass hills. Deirdre couldn't tell if the frogs chirped and the birds croaked or if it was just a trick of her own mind. She called out to one of them, and it squeaked back at her three times. Deirdre wondered if it was a greeting.

On walks to pick Wilde-Whites, Mr. Heart said hello to every animal he saw. He told Deirdre it was rude to not greet them, just as it was rude not to greet one's neighbor. Deirdre thought her father looked silly, waving enthusiastically at the furry-and-floppy-eared belps, bold-colored butterflies, and waddling ducklings. Mr. Heart also tried to have conversations with them before they scampered away.

Occasionally the conversations looked rather convincing. The animal would reply to his own "hello," and then Mr. Heart would say something like, "fine weather today" or "what lovely feathers you have." It was all small talk — the same small talk Deirdre had listened to in Marketfair at Farmer Hutch's stand.

Deirdre's attention slipped back to the present as the River Olde pulled the leaf along faster. She was becoming fond of her adventure. It was all very wonderful indeed. Had the knapsack not been left on the shore, this moment would have been perfect for a picnic. Although Deirdre still felt bad, somewhere between then and now, the guilt of leaving their snacks behind had lessened.

James sat up as the leaf began spinning in slow circles. "We're approaching Big Bend," he said confidently. "How long was I asleep?"

"Not too long," Deirdre replied as she attempted to brush her hair with her fingers. She was looking back towards Treliave, who was still visible beyond the hills they had traveled around.

Leaning over the edge of the leaf, James plunged his head into the water. As he pulled himself back up, he shook his head back and forth while laughing.

"Watch it," Deirdre said to him. With grass stains and wrinkles already on her tea party dress, she didn't want the addition of murky river water.

James didn't apologize but retorted, "You should try it. You won't look like such a bedhead."

Deirdre stuck her tongue out at him, which only made James laugh once again. He pulled the stem of the leaf and held it like a rudder so they'd stop spinning. Once steadfast, Deirdre could see what James referred to as Big Bend. It was, quite literally, a large water-rushing turn in the River Olde. There were several large stones protruding in different sections of the waterway. As they approached, the sound of the hurried waters grew to a roar, and there was the unmistakable sight of acrobatic fish doing synchronized backflips along the water's edge.

"Scared?" James inquired cheekily as he saw Deirdre's eyes widen.

"No," she returned, too hastily to sound genuine.

"I've sailed this river a hundred times… twice alone and blindfolded. You have nothing to worry about," James bragged.

"But have you ever crashed or fallen off?"

"Yes. It's just as fun."

This didn't help to settle Deirdre's nerves. She still couldn't swim. She tried inching back on the leaf as if to delay her imminent doom, but all too quickly she ran out of room to scoot. The roar of the rapids berated her ears.

Through the noise came James's confident storytelling voice. "One time," he said with a chuckle at his own thought, "I was on my way to the capital city to steal some sugar cubes from a friend of mine, Woodrow Usarenadale. He's an older person. A collar-maker." James leaned the stem to his right. "I was here on the water, napping like I just did, but forgot to wake up when I felt the spins. I was so caught up in my dreamscape that the River Olde tipped the leaf over. You'd think I would have woken up in my splash, but I didn't. I stayed asleep until I reached the docks of Auroval."

"This isn't a very good story," Deirdre said as the leaf suddenly jolted to the right. It sounded to her like James was lucky not to have drowned.

"It's not over yet," James said, but Deirdre wasn't sure if he was speaking about his story or their ride through Big Bend. She opened her eyes and saw that they were heading straight for a rock.

"Look out!" she screamed.

James tugged on the stem and dodged the solid wall of stone by inches. His bold laughter signaled that this was his idea of fun. "So anyway. I washed up beside the dock. My leaf was gone, along with my shoes and the bowtie I had decided to wear. You have to dress your best when you show up unannounced at a collar's house." The water beneath the eldestleaf began to settle. The rapids fizzled, and James let out a sigh. "That was close," he remarked.

Deirdre warily opened her eyes.

"I stole Woodrow's sugar cubes and later learned that the water in my pockets turned them into a sugary mush."

Deirdre's stomach grumbled. "I'm hungry," she said.

"We'll pull over for the night in a moment. I know a spot where we can pick berries and popcorn for dinner."

"The night?" Deirdre exclaimed with a quivering voice. "I have to be home before bed." When she had looked at the Adventure Map with James, the plan had seemed quick and simple. The map had teased her into believing that the adventure would only last an afternoon. Deirdre imagined her parents searching for her all over Bellebrook, and now they would spend another night looking for her. The Whitesals and the Perkins would have helped. Then the town would have gathered today to search in the Farwood and south along the Little Fields.

"We will reach Mill Pond in the morning," James said casually. "Dark waters aren't safe, even without Sea Monsters."

The warmth from the sun began to chill as it sank behind the trees to the south, laying its evening blanket across the land. Treliave had receded from view. Deirdre still had mixed feelings about the eldestree, but a part of her would have been comforted by its looming figure.

James watched Deirdre adjust her posture with the hopes of catching a glimpse of Treliave's tallest branches between the hilltops. When James had been younger and first gathered the courage to leave Treliave, he would turn around every few feet to make sure she didn't uproot and move. When he had finally made it to the valley of the River Olde, he'd duck down so that she vanished from sight, only to leap back up to make sure she was still watching him. Over time James learned that Treliave would always be where she stood. She never left. This was why, unlike Deirdre, James didn't mind her disappearance. Instead, he whistled a cheerful tune until the waterway became too dark. Then he guided the raft back to shore.

The leaf sailed into a woodland shoreline where a pocket of soft grass, berry bushes, and plump wild cornshrubs lined the perimeter.

Hopping off the leaf, James turned around to offer Deirdre a hand — her knees had become wobbly from the long afternoon of floating.

"Happy landing," he told her as she nearly tumbled into his arms. When Deirdre finally found her footing, James smiled and said, "Here's the plan." He stressed the final word as if to appease her. "You pick the berries — purple ones — while I make the beds and gather the popcorn."

"How come you're doing so much and I'm not?"

James frowned. "Do you know what mellomoss is?"

"No."

"Do you know how to size a blanket?"

"No."

"What's the difference between ripe wildcorn and a dud?"

"Okay." Deirdre huffed. "You don't have to act like such a know-it-all."

James shook his head. "But I do know it all. Just pick as many berries as you can and bring them over there." He pointed towards the center of the clearing.

"I won't be able to carry much without a basket."

"Well, use your shirt."

Deirdre looked down. "You mean my dress?"

"Yes, that."

"But the berries will stain it."

"So?" James replied as he rolled a relatively large rock onto the eldestleaf. The last thing he wanted was to be stuck on the edge of the River Olde without a boat.

"So, my dress will be ruined," Deirdre said, flabbergasted by his indifference.

"You'll have to decide," James sighed. "Either go to sleep hungry or get your dress dirty." He walked to the edge of the clearing and the rows of wild cornshrubs.

Alone in the clearing, Deirdre stood with her arms crossed tightly across her chest. Then she marched herself to the nearest berry bush. With daylight fast diminishing, it was difficult for her to see which berries were blue and which ones were purple. She cupped as many as she could in her hand before walking to the center of the clearing. Deirdre dropped them in a small pile. Her stomach growled again.

The sound of her hunger rumbling echoed back from the forest. Deirdre stopped. She scanned the edges of the woods with fright. "James?" she called out, but the boy didn't reply. Balancing a handful of berries, Deirdre walked back towards her pile. A third of her collection had vanished. "James?" she called out a second time. "This isn't funny."

Another grumble echoed from the trees. "Stop it!" Deirdre snapped. "I don't like pranks." She waited a moment before shaking off as much fear as she could. Darkness now covered the clearing, and the colors of the berries were harder to distinguish. Deirdre plucked one and popped it in her mouth.

"Bleh, yuck!" she sputtered after coughing up the sour taste of a blueberry.

"Bleh, yuck!" echoed the forest.

Deirdre leapt to her feet and scanned the edge of the woods again. She felt something brush past her and dart across the clearing. Spinning around, Deirdre saw nothing — not even her pile of collected berries. "James!" she hollered desperately, now wishing he'd just return,

"What?"

"Where are you?"

James appeared with odd bundles beneath each of his arms. "Right here," he said. "You didn't pick any berries?"

"I did," Deirdre snapped, her eyes darting back and forth. "Something's here. A monster. We should go."

James dismissed her suggestion with a wave of his hand.

"Nonsense," he said. "There aren't any monsters here, and even if there were…" He gave his wooden sword a pat. "… I'd take care of it." James tossed the bundles where the pile of berries had been, then unrolled them like sleeping bags.

"This is mellomoss," he told Deirdre. "It's the softest bedding you can get in these woods. It grows fluffiest on rocks, but mellomoss from a log is comfy too. It'll also keep you warm at night."

"How did you get it?"

"What do you mean?"

"Doesn't moss stick to the rocks and logs?" Deirdre asked, fighting the urge to watch the tree line.

"You just tickle it by the corners and peel it off," James said. "Lay down and give that one a try."

Deirdre did so, and to her surprise, she found the mellomoss quite soft. It felt just like her bed at home.

"Oh! And if you fluff up the corners you can shape the top portion into a pillow." James demonstrated with his own unrolled layer of moss.

When Deirdre stood up, James stepped into the center of a patch of tall grass. "One, two, three, four," he said while drawing a large rectangle. A thin, silvery mist outlined the perimeter of James's drawing. The moment he hopped out of the way, the grass rose and started to weave itself together. "One, two, three, four," he repeated. The woven layers of grass separated from the ground, leaving rectangular patches of dirt exposed.

"That's how you size blankets?" Deirdre asked.

"Yes," James said, patting off little clumps of earth. "This grass isn't the best, but it will do the trick."

Deirdre's stomach grumbled, and the forest grumbled back. "Did you hear that?" she said quickly. Her eyes were fixed on the shadowed trees again.

"Nope," James replied. He was too preoccupied with the dirt on his own blanket. Once both were dubbed "clean enough," he carefully laid them on top of the mellomoss beds. Then James ushered Deirdre over towards the wild cornshrubs. They were fat and grew low to the ground, quite unlike the cornfields Deirdre had seen in her hometown. She watched as James tore open a husk, revealing a single oval-shaped kernel that was closer in shape to a watermelon than a traditional cob.

"How do you eat this?" Deirdre said skeptically.

"Well, it's the kernel," James explained. "In order to pop it, you just have to do this."

He picked up the kernel with both of his hands, brought it close to his mouth, and huffed a breath of warm air onto it. Without warning, the large seed made a resounding *POP*. Deirdre jumped back in surprise. A single piece of popcorn, the size of a large pumpkin, appeared in James's hand.

"Can I try?" Deirdre asked.

"Of course," James answered mid-bite. "Make sure the corn is slightly yellow and not red or brown. Those are the duds."

Deirdre nodded before splitting a husk open. It took her two tries before finding a light-yellow kernel. Bringing it up to her lips as James had done, she sighed warm air onto it and *POP*. Deirdre let out a snort of excitement. James applauded, and Deirdre took a triumphant bite. The crown was just as salty and buttery as the popcorn her parents made on the stovetop at home. For a moment, Deirdre forgot about the monster lurking in the woods, but only for that one moment. As she opened her mouth for a second bite, something, other than a kernel, popped. Deirdre looked up.

The sound echoed over and over again. Deirdre didn't know what to do other than yelp and hide behind James.

The last rays of daylight faded. "I told you there was a monster!" Deirdre squealed as James dropped his popcorn and reached for his sword. Dozens of dark figures floated down from the lowest branches of the trees — popping and gurgling louder and louder as they hovered closer and closer.

-X-

WIZ CATCHING

James waited. He squinted through the darkness with his wooden sword drawn and his feet planted firmly on the ground. Deirdre remained hidden behind him while he considered the floating figures. The popping sound was bothersome, but it wasn't scary. "Ha-ha!" James shouted as if to mock the monsters.

"Ha-ha!" the monsters mimicked in reply.

"He-he-he!" James said as a smile spread across his face.

"He-he-he!"

"Ho-ho-ho?"

"Ho-ho-ho?"

"What are you doing?" Deirdre hissed.

"They aren't monsters," James whispered to her. "Stand perfectly still and don't move until I say so. We're about to play a game." Suppressed excitement hung in James's tone.

"Ho-ho-ho?" the monsters sounded again.

Deirdre felt as though a hundred or more unknown beasts were closing in on them. She fought hard to remain still as James had instructed.

"Ready?" he asked, slowly placing his sword on the ground. "Set." He crouched down, ready to pounce on whatever was surrounding them. "WIZ!" he screamed at the top of his lungs.

Across the dark glen, the floating monsters burst into bright neon globes. Deirdre had to shield her eyes from the flash, but she glimpsed several dozen floating things.

James howled with cheer as he leapt through the air and snatched one of the monsters. Deirdre watched as he wrestled with the thing for a moment on the ground before yelling, "Bonk!"

"What are they?" Deirdre gasped.

"They're Wizzes." James laughed while raising the creature he had wrestled — showing an unconscious ball of glowing green fuzz.

It has a star-tipped tail and large round eyes. The other wizzes were zipping around the clearing, making small hiccup noises every time they darted in a different direction.

"They won't stay long," James told Deirdre as he chased another one. He caught it with ease. Its eyes were blissful and blue. "They glow all night if you bonk them," he explained before bopping it on the head. The happy eyes closed, but the creature continued to smile stupidly.

"Doesn't it hurt them?" Deirdre asked in shock.

"Nah," James said and set the second wiz down on the grass. "Wiz!" he hollered again, making the wizzes shine remarkably bright once more. "Come on!" James bothered Deirdre. "This is my favorite game!"

Running around the clearing, the two children stretched up for the wizzes within their reach. The little glowing creatures hiccupped and zigzagged away from their grasping fingers.

"Bonk!" James shouted for a third time as he smashed his fist on the top of another wiz. Deirdre kept her focus on just one wiz, which tormented her by sticking its tongue out every time she missed grabbing it.

"Come back here," she said through gritted teeth.

"Here! Here! Here!" the wiz mimicked.

"I got another," James announced from across the glen, shaking the fourth unconscious wiz. "How many have you got?"

"None," Deirdre growled mid-jump.

"Here! Here! Here!"

"Well, hurry up," James pressed. "They're starting to get smart and leave. Wiz!"

The creatures froze for a moment to illuminate. Deirdre seized her moment and grabbed the wiz she had been chasing.

"Nice!" James called. Deirdre raised her fist and was about to bonk it when the wiz looked up at her. She noticed purple smudges around its mouth and a blue discoloration on its tongue. This wiz had eaten the berries she had picked. It was babbling and cooing incoherently while it waited for Deirdre to bonk it. It wasn't afraid but grinning as stupidly as the others had before being knocked out.

"Just thump the top of it," James said. He grasped a wiz in each hand and bonked them together.

Deirdre balled her hand into a fist again but couldn't bonk the wiz she had caught. Even if the ball of fluff had stolen her pile of berries, she felt guilty at the thought of inflicting pain on it. There were enough bonked wizzes lining the mellomoss beds. Turning her back to James, Deirdre loosened her grip.

"Biz," the wiz peeped. It hovered for a second, bounding its star-tipped tail. Then it turned away and headed back towards the forest.

"Couldn't bonk it?" James inquired as Deirdre walked towards the cornshrubs.

"We had enough already," she explained as she picked up another yellow kernel. Exhaling onto it, Deirdre felt the corn pop. She tossed it to James, knowing he also hadn't had much to eat. James skewered the corn with his sword and ate it like a kebab. Deirdre popped another kernel for herself before sitting down on her mellomoss bed.

For a long while, they ate in silence. The shadows of the woods no longer scared Deirdre now that she was surrounded by the soft glow of wizzes. Beyond the edge of their campsite, she watched the Crystal moon's light dance along the River Olde. The moon itself was hidden from view, but the beams alone made Deirdre feel a little closer to home.

"Are you having fun?" James asked as he finished his corn.

"Yes," Deirdre answered. "Are your adventures always like this?"

"They usually start out this way."

James laid back on the mellomoss. He was searching for the final red hues of the Blood Moon. Its diminishing light marked the end of heatspell, the end of warm-weather adventures.

Deirdre waited patiently for him to continue. When it became clear that he was not going to elaborate, she asked, "Do you get lonely?" She tried to imagine having adventures as grand as this on her own. Who would she talk to? Where would she go?

"Nah, I have friends everywhere I go," James said. Questions like these were un-fun to him. He wanted to talk about simpler things. "Do you have a middle name?" he asked.

Deirdre nodded as she wiped crumbs from her mouth. "It's Rose."

"Rose?"

"Like the flower."

"A flower rose?"

Deirdre tilted her head in confusion. "You don't know what a rose is?"

James shook his head innocently.

Deirdre wasn't surprised. There was so much about James's extravagant life that she could not figure out that it only seemed right that he didn't understand her boring life in Bellebrook. Nevertheless, roses were her favorite flower. How tragic not to know what roses were? "They're the most beautiful smelling flower," Deirdre told him. "My father always gets me a yellow rose on my birthday."

"A yellow rose," James repeated with a smile. "I would like to see one of these flowers someday. Do you miss your mom and dad?"

"I've never been away from them for more than one night." She knew James didn't have any parents, but the thought that this was normal for him felt strange to her all the same. "Do you remember your parents?"

"I don't think I ever had them to begin with," James said flatly.

"No parents ever?" Deirdre knew where babies came from. She knew people didn't just pop out of the ground.

"I have no memory or piece of them to prove they ever existed."

"What about that box on your shelf?"

James rolled over to face her. "What about it?"

"What if it was a gift from your parents?"

"That's a silly thought. Why would parents give me a box, one that I can't even open?"

Deirdre felt sorry for James. She figured it was hard not having parents, but to not even know if they existed? It was unfathomable.

"Treliave raised me," James stated with pride. "It's always been me and my tree."

"I'm sorry."

"That's a silly thing to be sorry about."

Deirdre studied James's smile. "I guess it is," she agreed.

James bit his lip in thought for a moment. "Tell me more," he demanded.

"Tell you more about what?"

"About your parents."

Deirdre blushed and began to feel awkward. She didn't want to sound as if she was gloating, but since she couldn't think of a way to change the topic, she accepted his request. "My papa has brown hair and hazel eyes. He has the best voice for bedtime stories, and a scruffy beard that tickles when he kisses my cheek. He was the first guest to my tea party." Deirdre grinned as she fell into memories. "His hands always smell like dirt — dirt for, like, flowers in pots. And his favorite color is purple."

"That's a girl's color!" James laughed.

"Not dark purple," Deirdre defended. "He loves my mother, and me, and Pup."

"Who's Pup?"

"My pet kitten."

A crinkle in James's eyes gave away that he had no knowledge of pets, but Deirdre was too lost in her own thoughts to explain what a "pet" was.

"My mother is brave. She's tough and always expects me to be on my best behavior. And she gives the best hugs. Anytime I'm sad or scared or sick, her hugs always make me feel better again. I have blonde hair like her. Dad says I have her smile too, but I don't think so."

James cocked his head to the side. "Why?"

Deirdre lost focus and took a moment to reply. "Why what?"

"Why don't you have your mother's smile?"

"Well, for one thing… I'm not a mother. Mothers have several special smiles. One to make you feel safe. One to make you feel special. And one to make you feel all the love your heart can handle." Deirdre offered James a crooked smile. "I don't have those smiles."

James chewed on his fingernails, considering this, but in the end he shook his head with a sigh. "Maybe not, but you have your own smiles." He spat a fingernail into the grass. "And they're good smiles. I like them." He rubbed his nose on one of his sleeves with a sniff. The soft glow of bonked wizzes illuminated James's abandoned sword in the grass. He retrieved it and tucked it beside his bedding. "Your mother's smile sounds nice."

"Yes," Deirdre said.

James pulled his blanket over himself. "I'll do my best to get you back to them," he told her. "I'll take you home, Deirdre Yellow-Rose Heart."

Deirdre didn't correct him. She answered him with one of her own smiles and then tucked herself beneath her own blanket. "Thank you," she said softly before resting her head on the mellomoss pillow. As sleep slowly washed over her, Deirdre began to feel the comforts of home surround her. The grass-woven blanket began to feel like her pink, plush, cotton comforter. The little mound of moss warped into her feather-filled pillow. The sound of nature faded, and for a split second between sleep and consciousness, Deirdre believed she had traveled home. She imagined the smell of vanilla candles her mother enjoyed lighting, the distant ticking of a grandfather clock, and the delicate pitter-pattering of Pup playing with yarn.

In her mind, she pictured her room, her tea party table, a rocking chair, and her nightstand. Deirdre walked across the wooden floor and ran her fingertips over the smooth wall. There was no mistake, Deirdre missed her home, but the longer she fought to stay, the colder she began to feel. Dark shadows distorted the dream. Gray dust gathered beneath her fingers as if the room had gone untouched for ages. She involuntarily curled her body inwards as the fear of never returning knotted her stomach.

"Here," peeped a wiz.

Deirdre became aware of her own sleepy stirrings.

"Biz," peeped the wiz as it nuzzled her cheek.

Deirdre opened her eyes in time to see the blueberry-stained tongue lick the tip of her nose. Lifting a portion of her blanket, Deirdre welcomed the little ball of fuzz into her bed. She turned her head to see if James was asleep, only to discover he was gone. Without sitting up, Deirdre looked around. It was between light and shadow that she saw him sitting on a branch high up in one of the nearby trees. His head was resting against the trunk. James was gazing up towards the stars. Perhaps he had just had a bad dream too, Deirdre thought before drifting off, or maybe, he prefers to sleep in trees.

"Biz," the wiz suggested, and Deirdre agreed. She could ask him in the morning. Without another worry, she went back to sleep.

-XI-

THE RAEF FAMILY

Morning arrived with a cloudless blue sky and a blazing bright sun. The night's chill lingered in the early breeze, which had enough strength to carry the scent of the Aramayus. Dew covered the grass around the small clearing and began to dribble aimlessly towards the River Olde. As Deirdre sat up to wipe the sleep from her eyes, she caught a glimpse of James picking a shirt-full of purple berries.

"Good morning!" he said cheerfully.

"Good morning," Deirdre returned while scratching her head. She looked down at the wrinkles and her dress and sighed. Dresses weren't supposed to be slept in, let alone be worn several days in a row. Shivering as she kicked off her blanket, Deirdre looked around the glen with sleepy puzzlement.

"What's wrong?" James asked.

"The wizzes, they're gone."

James chuckled. "Yes, they always leave before sunrise. I never know where they head off to." He spilled out the pile of collected berries for Deirdre to nibble. Then he gathered the grass-woven blankets and returned them to their muddy rectangular patches. The grass unraveled back into the earth.

"Did you sleep well?" Deirdre asked.

"I did. You?"

Deirdre nodded as she patted the sides of her coat. Both mittens and the windstone were still tucked away in her pockets.

James tugged on some loose wines and used them to tie up the mellomoss. "Just in case we have to go another night. Once we get to Mill Pond and the Great Road, this stuff can be hard to find."

"I saw you in the tree last night," Deirdre blurted out, unable to retain her moment of collectedness.

"Oh."

"Why were you up there instead of in your bed?"

James shrugged. "I was just having one final think before going to sleep."

"A think?"

"It's impossible to sleep until you've made your thoughts sleepy," James rationalized before tossing a handful of berries into his mouth. "Without the knapsack, we don't have much to eat. Then I thought of Mill Pond and the Harvesting Hills. They've got plenty of food there. Real food. Real breakfast. You know, so we can fill up before we continue our adventure."

"Lead the way!" Deirdre exclaimed. The idea of a real breakfast was too good to stray back to questioning James about his late-night tree-thinking.

Once James removed the boulder off their eldestleaf, he and Deirdre pushed it back into the water with ease. Deirdre climbed in first, crossed her legs, and looked ahead to where the River Olde broke free from the surrounding woodlands. James hopped in a step later and steered them towards the center current. It was at this point he began to sing:

From the Aramayus blue water flows
Through the River Olde it goes,
It passes east from Big Bend's round
And ends in Atloria's northern sound.

These waters are older than you or I,
They've seen the world both low and high
As storms, as snow, as fog, as hail
If water is history, this river's a tale.

"What's that from?" Deirdre inquired.
"Oh, it's a fisher's song from Blaemede."
"Do you know more?"
James smiled and continued:

There once was a fair, fearsome Captain
Who raided and plundered by sea.
She rode upon a skyserpent's back
With her crew — the Scourge of Black Tree.

They attacked under the cover of moonlight
And were gone before the first signs of day.
They torched all the towns,
For treasures abound,
And buried it far, far, away.

Then the Sovereigns raised ships to go hunting
For the Captain who sailed through the skies.
A hundred white sails, had set out to prevail,
But were burned red at the stroke of midnight.

It's been a hundred and three years in counting.
And the Captain has since not been seen.
Though no signs of plunder,
Some sailors now wonder,
If her hull has been claimed by the sea.

Deirdre clapped until James took a bow. The green hills and thin woodlands slipped away behind them and the open expanse of Elderland appeared. Long rolling fields sprawled in large squares, stitched together by villages along the river. Away in the distance, and almost too far to see, Deirdre spotted the shimmering white marble spires of a grand city. "That's it!" she said excitedly. "That's Auroval."

"Yep!" James said.

"Oh, please, can we go?"

"I thought you wanted to go home," James replied with an unsuppressed smile.

Deirdre frowned, straining her neck to keep the city in her sights. "Next time?"

"Sure." James kept his answer short because unless she wanted to help him steal sugar cubes, there wasn't much fun to be had in Auroval.

Then the Harvesting Hills came into view. Deirdre saw dark overturned soil and rows of crops.

"You're lucky to be arriving on the eve of the Harvesting festival. It's the greatest time to visit Mill Pond. I was going to come anyway, but that was before I knew you'd be coming with." James told Deirdre.

"What's the Harvesting festival?"

"It's a town-wide celebration for the return of the Crystal moon."

Deirdre frowned. "That's in the spring — after the Frost moon."

"No. It's today, before the rise of the Frost moon. There's no harvest to celebrate in the springtime. Nothing has grown yet."

"Well, in Bellebrook, we celebrate the Crystal moon's return in the spring."

James wasn't going to be misled by a girl who had never attended a Harvesting festival. "They have the best red berry pie, the sweetest carrot cake stew, endless barrels of pumpkin-apple cider, and these little flakey bread rolls that are smothered in butter." James smacked his lips in excitement. "The vegetable soup has every vegetable you can imagine in it, and it will fill you up so fast that you won't be able to eat more than one bowl of it. Oh, and if a guy named Bartyseed offers you a slice of chocolate cake, and you don't want it, you can give it to me. Of course, I'd tell you to have it politely, but if you offered it again, then I would take it and not give it back because it is so yummy."

Deirdre giggled at James's growing excitement. Everything he had just described sounded incredibly delicious to her. She hoped there would be enough time to attend the festival and be home before bed.

As the eldestleaf floated into an offshoot of the River Olde, it washed into a pond. One long rickety wooden dock stretched out to greet the children, and just beyond it stood a cluster of little farm-styled homes. Nearly all of them were painted a traditional barn red, with a few others colored light brown, and white. The rooftops were made of fresh golden straw or mismatched shingles. There were tall-leaning brick chimneys and flower-filled window baskets for every home. Cobblestone and mud roads twisted casually upwards from a pair of docks. In the center of the town was a stone fountain shaped like a cornucopia. Water poured from a spout into a low, round basin.

An old ramshackle mill, the namesake of the town, was erected on an island at the opposite end of the rickety bridge. Slabs of wood were nailed messily into chunks of the mill's siding like the patchwork on Mr. Button's other jacket. Although the mill appeared to be neglected, Deirdre couldn't help but admire it and the charming sounds it made as water rotated through its great wheel.

"Here we are!" James said as the eldestleaf gently folded up against the docks. He offered Deirdre a hand as she stepped up, and then he tied the stem to a piece of rope.

"It's so peaceful and quiet," Deirdre said absentmindedly. The farming town was more rustic and worn in comparison to Bellebrook. Paint chipped off window shutters and siding. The morning sun touched upon different shop signs. There was Bartyseed's Bakery, Piera Petal's Flower Boutique, Smithman's Repair Shop, and The Day's End Inn and Tavern.

The bell above a library chimed as James and Deirdre walked towards the town's fountain. "How now town plow?" James called towards an elderly man.

"Chow now brown cow," the man returned hastily. In his left hand, he clutched a large shepherd's cane. Tapping it twice upon the ground, a thin wisp of white pollen wafted over James and Deirdre. A spacious and toothy grin broadened the man's expression. "Who's your lady?"

Still leading Deirdre up the road, James turned around and replied, "Another adventurer." Deirdre spun around to wave at the man, but to her surprise, he wasn't looking at them. His eyes were glazed over, and he leaned heavily on his cane. She still gave him her most impressionable smile while adding a clear "Hello."

The man adjusted his gaze and returned with a wave. Then he walked back into the library.

"That's Mr. Averwood, the town storyteller and librarian."

"Is he blind?"

"Yes," James said.

"How is he the librarian if he can't see?"

"He usually has his son help him, but most of the people around here are too busy working their farms to read. The fields don't till themselves."

"And what were you two saying when you greeted each other?"

James pulled on his hair. "I'm Brown Cow." He then hunched his back and pretended to be an old man. "He's Town Plough." When Deirdre nodded, James then concluded, "I asked him what he was doing, and he replied that he was going to eat some breakfast. He likes to challenge people to a game of words."

"So, people don't actually speak like that in Mill Pond?"

"No. That would be crazy."

Deirdre sighed with relief. Having experienced plenty of crazy in the past two days, she would have almost accepted a town filled with people who only conversed in rhymes.

As James and Deirdre passed more homes and shops along the main street of Mill Pond, more people began to open their windows and doors. Some greeted James, while others eyed him suspiciously.

At the far end of the town square, James conjured a small orb of silver pollen. He aimed for a window on the second floor of a stone-stacked home.

The pollen flew up and splattered like a snowball against the shutters. A moment later a boy their age pushed the shutters open and looked out of his window, dazed and confused. He squinted through the bright morning sun. "James?" he called down groggily.

"Tasker!" James replied out loud. "I've come for breakfast."

The boy in the window wiped a booger from his nose and then

leaned out of his window a little further. He wore blue pajamas and a long, white sleeping cap. Trying to make sense of the girl standing beside James, Tasker grumbled something about the sun and disappeared.

Faint shouting echoed through the house before a series of feet stomping down steps. Tasker opened the door to his home a moment after. He had removed his sleeping cap but was still dressed in his pajamas. Ignoring Deirdre entirely, he looked at James and said, "Who's she?"

"This is Deirdre. We're on an adventure," James informed him.

"Are you here for the Harvesting Festival?" he managed to ask through an elongated yawn.

"Yes!"

Tasker shifted his mouth around as if tasting something from the previous night. He then offered his first welcoming smile and said, "I'll go wake Mum and Da' and have them make breakfast. Wait here." He shuffled back upstairs, the soft pattering of his bare feet retreating as he went.

Deirdre turned her back to the stairs with crossed arms and asked heatedly, "Who's he?"

James stared fondly after his friend. "That's Tasker Raef. He's my best friend."

The Raef home was one of the oldest structures in town. It was built out of gray stones pulled from the Harvesting Hills. Thick wooden beams crossed above to support the second level. Hammered into the beams were old nails and hooks, which held pots, pans, and dried spices. Compared to Deirdre's home in Bellebrook, the Raefs lived in a small house. The first floor was nothing more than an oversized kitchen with various chairs and cushions scattered against the walls. There was a large oak table resting in the center dressed in tattered tablecloths and two tarnished candle holsters.

There was fresh wood stacked in a wicker basket beside a simple brick fireplace. A brass cricket was crouched on the mantle. Deirdre could see the last orange coals from an old fire winking beneath a heap of gray ash. This house was new to her, but she felt somehow a part of it.

A minute later Tasker returned with his parents. Mrs. Raef was a slender woman with mousy features and high cheeks. She greeted James and Deirdre with a warm simile. "Happy Harvesting Day," she said to them. "You must have had a long trip here. Take a seat." She then turned towards Tasker. "Tass, would you stack some fresh wood in the fireplace?"

Mr. Raef grunted an irritated "hello" to James and, much like his son, neglected Deirdre's presence altogether. None of this was her fault, but this had not been the first time James had shown up too soon after daybreak. Usually, Mr. Raef was awake and about to head out to work in his fields, but since today was the Harvesting Festival, he had been hoping to enjoy a few extra hours of sleep.

"Mum, Mr. Raef, this is Deirdre," James told them. "It's okay that she has breakfast too, right?"

"Of course." Mrs. Raef laughed. She looked at James. "Where have you been these past few weeks? I was getting worried."

"Up and down the River Olde," James replied. He smiled at her with two perfect rows of teeth.

Mrs. Raef pulled a small pollen pouch from a peg above her. She tossed a pinch of its shimmering contents towards the fireplace. The logs Tasker had stacked in the fireplace ignited instantly. "Staying out of trouble?"

"Always," James said. His smile widened even further.

Mr. Raef scoffed while scratching his chin through an untamed black beard. "So you're here for the festival, eh?" Mr. Raef eyed the wooden sword strapped to James's side.

"Yes, sir."

"Not off to go fight Mountain Men or the Frost Bulls to the north?"

"Mountain Men?" Deirdre interrupted.

Mrs. Raef shot her husband a sharp look for starting such talk in front of their newest guest. "There's no mountain men, darling."

"There are too!" Tasker interjected. "Da' told us about them. He told James and me the story about the Mountain Men."

Fueled by his son's excitement, Mr. Raef sat up a bit straighter and said, "They exist, but they're no threat to any of us. They've been asleep for hundreds of years."

"Would you like cinnamon and sugar in your porridge, Deirdre?" Mrs. Raef asked before narrowing her eyes at Mr. Raef. A pot had been hung over the fire.

"Yes, please," Deirdre answered politely.

Mr. Raef folded his arms. "So where have you recently been along the River Olde, James?" he asked in a weak attempt to change the subject from Mountain Men.

"Everywhere."

"Of course," Mr. Raef said.

Tasker kept staring at Deirdre. His eyes showed no signs of welcome. It was as if she had threatened him. Deirdre tried to ignore it, but Tasker had positioned himself across from her at the table. No matter where she turned, he made sure to follow.

"How did you meet James, Deirdre?" Mrs. Raef asked while setting five bowls of porridge on the table.

"He was an unexpected guest at my last tea party," Deirdre replied.

"A common habit not exclusively with us, I see," Mr. Raef remarked.

"Sounds boring," Tasker mumbled.

Deirdre blushed and refrained from saying more.

"She's an amazing host," James informed the room before shoveling porridge into his mouth. "We're trying to make our way back to Bellebrook. Are any of the merchant carts leaving today?"

Mrs. Raef shook her head. "None of the merchants travel on the day of the festival. It's the biggest night of our year. You'll have to catch one tomorrow." She paused and looked at her husband. "Ask Morris if he'll take them."

Mr. Raef nodded.

"Da', tell the Mountain Men story again," Tasker demanded, spewing porridge towards Deirdre's bowl.

With one eye fixed on Mrs. Raef and her cooking spoon, Tasker's father replied, "So long as Miss Deirdre here knows that this story is just a story, an old firetale at best."

Deirdre straightened her posture and composed her most fearless expression. Her own father had shared enough scary bedtime stories to inflate her conference. Politely blowing on a spoonful of porridge, she leaned forward attentively.

"Before we, the little people, discovered these lands, Mountain Men roamed these parts. Back then there were whole forests of eldestree. The world was bigger then. It was bigger and scarier, and far more dangerous."

Deirdre imagined a world full of Treliaves and humans of equal size.

Mr. Raef continued, "These Mountain Men used to fight against each other for sport. They'd uproot smaller trees as clubs and destroy whole forests in their brawls. They were little people eaters too — savage monsters that couldn't be stopped. But as the tale goes, when the Mountain Men had uprooted all the little trees, they started pulling on eldestrees. These trees, naturally, didn't like this. They waged war on the Mountain Men and pulled them down into the depths of the earth with their roots."

"Da', you forgot to mention their slimy spit and orange boogers the size of boulders! What about their warts that leaked pus the length of rivers, their leathery flat feet, and their mimblin' black hangnails?!" Tasker was wild in the eyes as if his father had ruined the whole story by sparing Deirdre from these details.

"This isn't polite table-talk," Mrs. Raef interjected quickly.

Tasker looked up at his mother in disbelief. "But Mum!"

"Don't fight your mother," Mr. Raef told his son. "Upset her enough and she might sell you to the Wayfarer Queen. She will turn you into a miniature mountain man with a wave of her hand, and you'll be too ugly to return home. We wouldn't love something that ugly."

"Jerry!" Mrs. Raef snapped. James was leaning over his breakfast, spoon held halfway to his mouth, as a smile curled across his face. He loved when someone else was in trouble with Mrs. Raef.

Tasker's father cleared his throat and concluded the story. "The Mountain Men lost. The last of the eldestrees toppled themselves to crush them. Only two giants were left to roam the empty lands. With nothing to wrestle, they laid themselves down and went to sleep. They slept so long that their tough skin dried up and turned to stone. Now they are our mountains."

Leaning his entire body over the table and out of his seat, Tasker planted his palms directly in front of Deirdre and said darkly, "One day they'll wake up again, and when they do, they'll gobble up tea party-hosting girls like you."

"Tasker!" Mrs. Raef yelled. She swatted him on the rear with her cooking spoon.

"Ouch!" Tasker cried. He sat down clumsily.

Mr. Raef stifled a laugh, but it wasn't fast enough. "Think it's funny, do you?" Mrs. Raef whacked her husband with the spoon as well. "He wouldn't be so rude if you didn't encourage him with your terrible stories."

Mr. Raef folded his arms as if to protect his pride but apologized for his behavior all the same. Tasker followed suit.

Turning with a quick smile, Mrs. Raef looked towards Deirdre. "So, where are you from?"

"Bellebrook," she replied.

Mrs. Raef paused. "That's quite a distance you've traveled."

Deirdre was hesitant to answer. She could see adult suspicion in Mrs. Raef's eyes. James didn't seem to notice, however, or he didn't care because he went on to state, "I introduced her to Treliave, and we've fought grumpaguls, and we've been sailing on the river."

"My word, do your parents know?" Mrs. Raef asked. She had seen the wrinkles and dirt on Deirdre's dress and knew all-too-well of the wealth that came from Bellebrook. No orphan ever came from a town like that. Blaemede, perhaps, but not Bellebrook.

Deirdre nodded. She didn't want to lie. "They know I'm safe, but…" She paused as her eyes fell on an ink bottle on the mantle. "May

I write them a quick letter?"

Mrs. Raef nodded warmly. "Of course you may." She brought a piece of parchment and quill over to the kitchen table.

"Thank you for the porridge," James said.

"Yes," Deirdre added. "It was delicious."

"Well, I hope my two fools didn't spoil your appetite," Mrs. Raef said as she glared at her son and husband.

Bending over the piece of paper, Deirdre began to scribble an apology to her parents, while trying to explain her situation in short. She had stated the letter formally with "Dear Mother and Father," as her teacher had taught her. However, her pent-up worries broke through, making her sentences stretch longer and messier.

Voices sounded from the town square outside. Their words were distorted by the walls of the Raef home, but the volume was enough to catch everyone's attention. Mrs. Raef peered out of the front window. "They're gathering, Jerry. It's time to set up for the festival."

Reaching the middle of her letter, Deirdre's sentences shifted from apologies to excitement. She wanted to share every detail of her adventure thus far with James — the boy who was keeping her safe and bringing her home. Deirdre explained the wondrous encounters with Treliave and a flock of wizzes.

Mr. Raef stood. "Tasker, stay out of trouble and away from the tents while the adults are setting up." He shot a quick look at James to make sure his son's friend heard him too. Then, after grabbing a large brown coat, Mr. Raef pecked Mrs. Raef on the cheek and left to join the crowd outside. Deirdre watched James mouth something to Tasker while Mrs. Raef had her back turned to them. Tasker scrunched his face in puzzlement; he was not very good at reading lips. James rolled his eyes before clearing his throat. "What was it you wanted to show me, Tasker?"

"What?" Tasker replied stupidly.

"That thing you were telling us about earlier. Before breakfast…"

"I wasn't telling —" Tasker grimaced silently as James kicked him swiftly in the shins. "Oh, right… that!" He twisted around in his chair to look at his mother. "Mum, is it alright if James and I go out back?"

Deirdre frowned. "And me," she said.

Tasker looked at her bowl of porridge. "You can't leave the table until you've finished your breakfast."

"Wait for your guest to finish eating, Tasker," Mrs. Raef answered. "Once she's done, then all three of you can be excused."

"Hurry up, then," Tasker grumbled.

Not wanting to waste time or make Tasker dislike her even more, Deirdre signed her letter with love and finished the rest of her porridge in four heaping spoonfuls. It was terribly unladylike of her, and she felt a bit embarrassed when Mrs. Raef remarked on how quickly she had finished.

Truthfully, Deirdre wanted to write more in her letter. She wanted to apologize again for running away and say that she had the windstone but felt safer keeping it. She wanted to explain why there was cookie dough all over the house. She wanted to tell them not to worry and that she missed them, but there wasn't time. Mrs. Raef watched as she folded the letter.

"You don't want to write more?"

"I'm okay, thank you. They know I'll be home soon. Can you send it?" Deirdre asked her.

Mrs. Raef frowned slightly. "You don't know how to send a letter?"

"I'm too young."

"Without having been to your house, I can't send it. A postman will be by in a day or two. We can send it then."

"I'll do it!" James exclaimed abruptly.

Tasker snorted. "You don't know how, James."

James reached for the letter. "I've seen it. I've been to her house."

Mrs. Raef looked from James to the folded note. "Okay," she said.

Hopping off his stool, James rubbed his hands together excitedly. "How do I do it?"

"Not fair," Tasker whined. "Why can't I learn?"

Deirdre would have agreed, but she was too thankful that the letter would get to her parents sooner.

Mrs. Raef tied back her hair and wiped her hands with her apron before taking the letter back. She looked at James. "You need to picture the house. Think of the town, the streets, and the details leading up to it. Think about how you traveled there. Try to hold all those memories in your mind and then create a path from those memories to this house."

James knitted his brows together in concentration.

"Do you have all of that in your thoughts?"

He bobbed his head up and down.

"Okay, now place those thoughts and memories into your pollen."

With a quick wiggle of his fingers and a smile, James created a silver cloud between his hands. Mrs. Raef dipped the letter into it and then walked to the front door. When she opened it, the voices from the crowd barged in.

"Let's see if you did it," she told James with a reassuring smile.

The letter dropped for a split second before floating lazily inside a silver cloud. It turned slowly, end-over-end. Mrs. Raef opened the door a bit wider until the letter floated away like a bubble.

"Well done," Mrs. Raef praised. Her expression turned quickly into confusion. Neither Tasker nor James was still sitting at the kitchen table. Deirdre's attention had been fixed on the letter; she too had missed the boys' escape. The back door hinges creaked. "Go on, now," Mrs. Raef told her with a laugh. "Before they get into trouble without you."

-XII-

INTO TROUBLE AND OUT OF SIGHT

A low barrier of piled stones separated the wild grass of Tasker's backyard from the brown overturned soil of the Harvesting Hills. Rows of corn, patches of pumpkins, and more gourds than Deirdre could name sprouted from the ground. She paused and teetered on the top of the wall while James and Tasker quickly scrambled over it.

Bellebrook only had little flower farms, and although Deirdre had seen a vegetable farm before, never had she seen fields as huge as those behind the town of Mill Pond. To her far right, she could see a well-groomed apple orchard.

"Get off the wall!" Tasker spat hotly.

"I'm just looking," Deirdre replied. She was trying her hardest to remain kind, but the boy wasn't making it easy.

"We're planning mischief. There's no time for looking."

James snapped at them both. "Keep quiet. I need to think." He started rubbing his temples and squeezed his eyes tight. Deirdre shot James an apologetic look, but Tasker remained indignant and grumbled something about girls wasting time. Ignoring him, Deirdre hopped off the wall and trotted over to James.

"Why doesn't he like me?" she asked.

"Doesn't? Of course he likes you," James replied.

"No. He's grumpy towards me."

"He's just focused on today's adventure."

Deirdre didn't believe James and began staring at Tasker in earnest. "Could he be full of grumpaguls?"

James now turned to look at his best friend, who happened to be picking his nose at that moment. Tasker paused. Noticing their looks, he removed his finger and wiped whatever he had dug up on his pajama bottoms.

"Bug flew up there," he explained, cheeks reddening by the second.

"Nah," James answered Deirdre. "Grumpaguls don't grow in children."

"What are you two talking about?" Tasker called.

James shifted so he could join them. "The Harvesting Festival."

Tasker sighed and looked wistfully back towards his town. Somewhere beyond his thatched roof, tents were being raised, tables were being arranged, and a large assortment of desserts were being baked.

"We need to get one of Bartyseed's cakes before the festival," James declared.

"You mean steal?" Deirdre asked disbelievingly. This was something she had never done, never considered, and had been raised knowing never to do.

"Yeah," James replied easily.

"But we could get into trouble!"

"Or we could get a whole chocolate cake just for us." Tasker rubbed his belly, foreseeing the chocolatey-bliss. Deirdre judged his self-control based on the tightness of his waistband. The drawstrings on his pants were knotted into the tiniest bow.

"I don't know," Deirdre said hesitantly. "Didn't your father say to stay away from the tents?"

"Bartyseed's Bakery isn't near the tents," Tasker scoffed as if answering Deirdre were a monotonous chore. He climbed up onto the same stone wall he had snapped at Deirdre for standing on. "How are we going to snatch it?"

"Sneakily," James answered. He was back to rubbing his temples and squeezing his eyes shut.

"Scared?" Tasker asked Deirdre.

"No," she shot back. "I was just thinking that perhaps there are better ways to prepare." Deirdre thought about all the bedtime stories her father had told her. She overcame Tasker's derision. "We need a diversion."

"A di-what?"

"We have one of those," James said confidently. He swung his sword around. "And we have me."

"Do you even know how to use that?" Deirdre asked suspiciously.

Tasker rejected her question disdainfully, "Of course he does. Just look at him!" They both watched as James ran ahead swinging wildly at the ends of cornstalks. He made whooshing noises with his lips and raspberry sounds with his tongue. When the cornstalks proved to be boring adversaries, James scooped up a stick and tossed it towards Tasker.

They fought along the top of the wall, laughing as they went. Deirdre raced along below them.

The playful duel continued all the way to the wall's end at the far corner of Mill Pond. James teetered on the last few inches, and Tasker made a strong jab with his stick. Whether it was on purpose or not was unclear to Deirdre, but James swayed to the side, grabbed Tasker by the arm, and pulled him off the wall. They both landed on the ground with a thud; Tasker hit the ground first.

"I win!" James crowed.

"You cheated," Tasker stated in disbelief.

"It's not cheating to fall off the wall second."

"But you pulled me."

"I took you down."

Tasker pouted as he tried to wipe smeared mud from the back of his pajamas. Deirdre looked down at her own dress. She was proud of herself for abstaining from the sword fight. Had she been the one to fall and earn a new patch of mud stains, her attitude towards the day would have darkened. And yet, had James offered her a swordstick, Deirdre secretly thought that she might have cared less for her dress in exchange for the excitement.

As the boys continued bickering about rules they had never established, Deirdre sank into a fit of worry. It had found her as abruptly as the ground had found Tasker's rear-end. Although a letter was currently floating towards Bellebrook, Deirdre was struck by the fear that her parents would not receive it. The reality of having to wait another day made her stomach churn. What would her parents say? Did her parents think she ran away on purpose? Would they still be searching for her? These thoughts tormented her. Deirdre's cheeks grew hot as her heart pounded inside her chest.

"Are you in?" James asked her. His voice had gotten louder as they walked between the few scattered homes on the outskirts of Mill Pond.

"What?" Deirdre had barely heard him.

"Are you in?"

Before she could fully comprehend the question, Tasker said, "Of course she isn't." Then in a stuffy and squeakishly high voice, he added, "Girls don't steal."

Deirdre rolled her eyes.

"See, she's about to cry," Tasker bullied.

"Stop it," she snapped back. "I'm in."

James beamed with excitement. "Brilliant." They turned towards the town square. Long wooden posts and great white sheets of fabric were being tied and pulled up as they arrived. Autumn-colored flags and ribbons were being tied along the wide stretches of rope between homes.

"Tag!" James shouted merrily, tapping Deirdre hard in the shoulder. "You're it!"

"Haha!" Tasker said in amusement.

Deirdre turned on the spot and chased after him.

James moved around a group of adults carrying heavy wooden

tables. He leapt from a chair onto a barrel drum, then grabbed an overhanging tree branch. He perched himself within it, happily watching the game he had started.

Tasker darted towards a stack of crates, but by the time Deirdre reached them, she had to wait for a line of adults to pull a wheelbarrow full of pumpkins past. Tasker dashed elsewhere. He headed for a collection of chairs stacked in tall columns. Deirdre raced after him.

"Watch it," shouted a voice.

"Careful now," called another.

Deirdre and Tasker ran through the streets, disrupting the people working hard to set up the festival. Other kids noticed them and suddenly were joining their game. They harassed Deirdre to chase them instead.

James leapt out of his hiding place and landed in front of her. The two of them stopped, staring in a standoff with delighted grins. Deirdre stretched out her arms as she guessed which way James would dart. The crowd of children gathered around them.

"You can't catch me," James taunted.

Deirdre heard Tasker snicker from somewhere close behind her. Her smile widened. "I can't what?"

"You. Can't. Catch. Me."

Deirdre waited for Tasker to snicker a second time. When he did, she spun around and reached out for him. Tasker was caught off guard. He stumbled back, but just before Deirdre could tag him, another girl leapt in between. "Tag!" Deirdre shouted before realizing what had happened.

A little girl with bouncy curls and a pair of bright orange overalls squealed in excitement and started chasing someone else. Tasker sighed in relief.

James grabbed Deirdre by the wrist. "Good job," he hissed excitedly. Then he tilted his head, indicating that Tasker should follow before leading them away from the game and towards Bartyseed's Bakery.

A large display window revealed an assortment of pastries unlike anything Deirdre had ever seen, but the sign on the door read: Closed. This didn't seem to bother James. He looked up at the second-floor windows, a small flat where George and Billson Bartyseed lived.

"I'm going to see if anything is cooling on the windowsill," James informed them as he sniffed the air. Tasker opened his mouth to protest—he wasn't going to be left behind to babysit a girl—but his friend took off without waiting to hear his complaints.

Deirdre crossed her arms firmly over her chest. Tasker leaned against the wall and shoved his hands deep into his pockets. Both of them kicked at pebbles on the ground, but they didn't talk. Deirdre would have enjoyed the silence had Tasker not been such a mouth breather.

"Can I help you?" inquired a portly man. His bald head glinted in the light of the early afternoon sun.

"No," Tasker answered rather rudely.

The man smiled as he lifted a bag of flour higher onto his shoulder. "This your lady-friend, little Raef?"

"NO!" Tasker shouted in abject horror.

"Who are you then, miss?" laughed the man as he searched for a key in his pocket. His eyes looked at Deirdre with sincere interest and care.

She replied with her name in an indisputably sweet tone.

"Pretty name. I'm Billson."

"You're the baker. I've heard all about your cakes."

Billson smiled but shook his head as he opened the door to the shop. "My George does the cakes. I bake all the bread."

Seeing that his hands were full, Deirdre tried to help by flipping the shop sign to "Open."

"Why thank you," he said through the sack of flour.

Tasker scowled at Deirdre, as this was not a part of the plan, but she ignored him.

The bakery air smelled of butter, sugar, vanilla, and nutmeg. Little clouds of powdered sugar and flour drifted in from the kitchen beyond.

"Georgy, I'm back!" Billson called as he dropped the burlap sack.

Deirdre was quickly distracted by the dessert cases filled with pastries. There were cupcakes dressed in autumn-colored icings lined neatly into rows. Thick blocks of brownies were stacked like step-pyramids, with globs of caramel and marshmallows. On a shelf above, there were personal-sized apple and pecan pies with the most impressive crust-made lacings. But once Deirdre caught sight of enchanted floating plates carrying a rainbow-assortment of macaroons, she craved only for that.

To Deirdre's side was a small rocking chair with a yellow cushion for customers to sit in. A wood-fire burner with a teakettle on top was cornered on the other side.

George's head poked through a gap in the wall that divided the kitchen from the shop. His head was topped with tightly wound curls, all pulled up into a bun.

"I see you brought a customer with you," he said with the same warm expression as Billson.

"This is Deirdre," his partner said.

"Deedra?" George said as he ambled out of the kitchen. He carried a beautifully sculpted, three-tiered chocolate cake. "Deedra, what?"

"Deirdre, from Bellebrook," she replied, ogling at the dessert in pure awe.

This answer was sufficient for the pastry chef as he wiped an excess of chocolate icing onto his apron. He reached out with a slightly cleaner hand. "Pleased to meet you, Deirdre from Bellebrook. What brings such a charming little lady like you to Mill Pond?"

"The Harvesting Festival," Deirdre replied succinctly. She pretended to try and see all the different pastries while peering through the glassless window to find the back windowsill James had gone searching for.

"A fine reason to come," Billson remarked. He scratched the back of his neck. "Where are your parents?"

Deirdre politely looked at George. "They're at home," she said.

"In Bellebrook? Surely, you didn't travel here all by yourself."

"She's with the Mayor's boy," Billson answered for her.

George squinted out the front window, identifying Tasker in his muddy pajamas. "Never knew Jerry and Ellie had family in Bellebrook."

"Oh no… I'm just a friend." Nausea chased the sentence up Deirdre's throat. She struggled to distinguish whether her reaction came from calling Tasker a "friend" or seeing James at that precise moment, standing in the back window. His mischievous brown eyes scanned the kitchen before finding Deirdre and giving her a conspiratorial wink.

Billson and George were busy watching Tasker and the other children. They shared a wishful look — as if they'd trade all the pastries in their shop for one of them, or more accurately, one of their own. Billson blinked. "How about a treat for helping me flip the sign?" he asked Deirdre.

"Yes," George agreed. He smiled at Deirdre. "Sit, sit, tell us about Bellebrook. Bill and I have always wanted to visit." Deirdre was ushered towards the rocking chair. Diverting her gaze, she was relieved to see James had vanished from the window. Perhaps, he had realized it wasn't safe to steal with both bakers in the shop. Deirdre's hands were suddenly cold and clammy. She wiped them on her dress.

"That needs a stitching," George said.

Deirdre nodded with embarrassment. Her mother would have never allowed her to look like this.

Billson returned from the kitchen with two additional chairs. On his way over, he plucked a macaroon free from an enchanted plate and gave it to Deirdre. It was the size of her whole fist.

"So your mother and father are back in Bellebrook. They let you travel here alone?"

"Oh no, another friend was coming to the festival, so they brought me." The lie sprung from her thoughts with uncanny ease. It was kind of exciting. Deirdre felt like a bedtime storyteller.

"Do you have any brothers or sisters?" George asked casually.

"No. It's just Pup and me."

"Pup?"

Deirdre replied through a mouthful of lemon-flavored macaroon, "My kitten."

Billson chuckled, and George's cheeks flushed as adult cheeks tend to do when children say something cute. Deirdre was so absorbed with the pastry in her hand that she didn't notice their reactions.

"What do your parents do?"

Deirdre paused to think. "They…" she began but then stopped. She understood George's question, but she had never asked her parents about their jobs. "They…" Deirdre stuffed her macaroon into her mouth to buy herself more time to think. "They host tea parties with me."

Billson nodded as if this were a respectable occupation while George gave him a look Deirdre didn't quite understand.

Not once, in all her memories, had Deirdre ever seen her parents "go to work" the way other parents did. They had always been home with her; cooking, gardening, cleaning, helping host tea parties or reading altogether in the living room.

CRASH! A metal clang broke the casual silence in the shop. Billson jumped to his feet and headed straight for the kitchen. "Hey!" he shouted. James was standing impishly on top of a counter with arms full of pastries. His brown hair lay askew, filled with bits of icing and sugar. The gleeful smile on his face, caked with gobbled desserts, looked utterly foolish.

"You, again!" George exclaimed.

Deirdre fumbled with her macaroon. It dropped onto the floor, scattering crumbs. She looked up again to see Billson grabbing a rolling pin. James tried to say something, but his cheeks were stuffed with gloating puffs of fried dough.

"Hand those over!" demanded George. He chased James around the kitchen.

James leapt off the counter and disappeared from Deirdre's view. All she could see was the anger and tumult of bakers.

Inclined to leave quietly, Deirdre stood. Her eyes drifted back to the chocolate cake. It stood, defenseless, on top of the display case where George had set it down. A crown jewel of unparalleled deliciousness, it beckoned her to take it. Deirdre's weight shifted between her left and right foot. One advised her towards the door, while the other urged her closer to the cake.

"Thieving little monster!" George shrieked.

James was swinging from a hanging rack of pots and pans. He was no longer devouring the stolen pasties, but rather pelting poor Billson and George as if they were grumpaguls. James laughed boisterously as if it were all a game.

Without recognition or warning — without thought, fear, or intention — Deirdre found herself holding the chocolate cake. She had balanced it carefully as she pulled it from the display case. It had teetered slightly on its plate and then rested heavily in her arms. Tasker, having heard the commotion through the kitchen window, had appeared by the door of the shop. He gawked as Deirdre crept towards him. The aroma of chocolate wafted around her nose as Tasker opened the door. The shouts from the bakers confirmed their continued distraction. The street outside, though full of people setting up for the festival, was too busy for her pillaging to be noticed.

"Away with you!" Billson roared. Deirdre looked back to see James diving out the window. Tasker hissed for her to keep moving. Guilt began to wash over her in a flood. A strong desire to return the cake caused her left heel to drag. James appeared at the far end of the street, and Deirdre knew there was no time left to return the cake. The door closed behind her and she, the Cake Thief, vanished from the shop.

-XIII-

WHISPERS OF ADVENTURE

"Splendorous!" James cheered as Deirdre and Tasker hurried down the street and into a tight alleyway. "You were the best double diversion I've ever seen!"

Deirdre, feeling less guilty as they rounded the corner, beamed. She had no words. Her arms were beginning to feel tired, but before she could voice this, Tasker asked, "Where are we gonna go?"

"In here!" James indicated excitedly, pointing towards a dingy-looking door. It was propped open with a brick and had a sign that read: Day's End Tavern, please use the front door.

"We aren't allowed in there," Tasker cautioned.

"Well, we can't go back out in the street. The Bartyseeds will know the cake has been stolen."

Deirdre bit her lip nervously. "What if we give it back?"

"Don't be stupid!" Tasker snapped. "We'll still get in trouble."

"Tasker's right," James said, licking his chops greedily. "We have to eat it now, so there's no evidence."

"H-here?" In the alleyway?" Deirdre stammered. Now she felt like a true criminal.

James shook his head and pointed towards the door a second time. "I'll check to see if it's empty." Pressing himself against the wall of the tavern, James slid to the edge of the doorframe. He listened for sounds of trouble. The cake began to tremor in Deirdre's hands. Tasker lifted the tray from her tiring grip.

"Thanks," she said with a sigh.

"I don't want to eat it off the ground," Tasker grumbled, but his tone was gentler than it had been.

James hissed at them. Shouts could be heard from the main street. George and Billson were looking for their cake and the girl who had stolen it. Tasker shuffled ahead of Deirdre, whose eyes were glued on the entrance of the alleyway. She backed herself towards the tavern door, fear and excitement giving her heartbeat a new rhythm.

"Come on," James urged. He tugged her by the arm, and they crept inside.

The Day's End tavern was not a place where Deirdre would have liked to end her day. The lighting was dim, with only one window beside the back door. Natural sunlight struggled to pass through torn fabric nailed to the wall as a makeshift curtain. It was dirty and thick with the scent of burnt cigars. Gnarled wood had been nailed over holes in the walls, evidently caused by brawling customers.

Deirdre's shoes stuck to the floor. It wasn't the kind of sticky sensation one might enjoy from a sweet shop like Bartyseed's, but a stickiness that revealed how infrequently the floor was scrubbed. A layer of grime peeled off the floor with each step, leaving a fresh set of footprints from the back entrance and through the kitchen.

"Wait," James instructed as the group paused behind a wall of beaded strings. It divided the back room from the front. The owner of the tavern was peering out his window, trying to understand the clamor being raised by his neighbors.

James pointed towards a table covered with a long-checkered cloth. As quietly as the stickiness of the floor allowed, the three children dashed over to it. Deirdre noticed that the bar still had dirty glasses and bottles strewn across its surface from the previous night. James lifted the tablecloth and Tasker entered first, anxiously balancing the cake. Deirdre followed, and James ended the procession. The door to the tavern burst open.

"Have you seen Tasker Raef, a little blonde girl, or a brown-haired boy?" gasped Billson in a voice filled with exhaustion and panic.

"Nope," returned the tavern owner.

"They swiped one of George's cakes."

"A whole cake, swiped, how?"

"The boy… he… she… we…"

James and Deirdre were listening attentively. Tasker, on the other hand, was keeping quiet by stuffing handfuls of chocolate cake into his mouth.

"Well, if I see them, I'll let you know," the tavern owner said.

Billson Bartyseed left just as his partner's shouts resounded back from the tents being raised. The tavern owner chuckled softly to himself as he returned to cleaning empty glasses.

"Eat up," James whispered. He reached for the cake with one of his own grubby hands.

Deirdre hesitated. She had accidentally touched the floor; the grimy, ale-stained, cigar-smelling floor. Her skin crawled. She needed to wash her hands before touching the cake, but she knew that would be impossible. Tasker pulled another chunk from the chocolate tower between them, his eyes radiating happiness. He closed his fist around the chunk of cake, squeezing it through his fingers, and then licked the mush that seeped out.

James sucked each fingertip before seizing a second piece. Tasker wiped his mouth on his sleeve. Deirdre felt nauseated as she slowly reached towards the chocolate cake. The faces of her High Sociotea guests appeared in her mind. They were repulsed by her stooping so low.

The moist cake collected under her fingernails first. Then it rose around and between her fingertips. Deirdre winced as the icing coated her palm. Pulling a piece away, she brought it to her lips and took her first bite. The taste was beyond her comprehension.

James smiled through a mouthful of chocolate as he watched Deirdre's eyes widen. Tasker was no longer wasting time by eating with one hand. He scooped out whole portions of cake to bury his face in, snarfing as much of it down as he could.

The door to the tavern swung open and three pairs of worn traveling boots appeared. The children froze.

"Two each, Frank," said a voice.

"One for me, two will be too much," corrected a second voice. It sounded vaguely familiar to Deirdre; deep and estranged from the typical accents of Riverbed. Still poking the last bit of cake into her mouth, she peered out under the fringes of the tablecloth. The daylight from the doorway obscured any details of the customers. All she could see were the bottoms of their cloaks, which were colored deep blue, brown, and purple.

"You've traveled a long way," said the first voice that had entered and ordered drinks. Deirdre continued to watch the boots as they nudged chair legs out from under a nearby table. The bottom edges of the cloaks then rested in lazy folds.

"We've only just come from Marketfair," replied the second man. Although Deirdre could not see their faces, she vaguely recognized the voice.

"Where's your caravan?"

"On the outskirts."

"Would you like to settle it closer to town?"

The second man shifted as if to look at the third guest. "That won't be necessary." For a moment, the customers remained silent. The tavern owner appeared from behind his counter. Five glasses clunked heavily on the table.

"To old friends from afar," toasted the first man.

"To a fair trade," answered the second man, and Deirdre placed his voice instantly; Lazarus the Wayfarer.

Three glasses clinked.

"Did you bring the bracelets, Balis?" asked the third patron.

Deirdre froze. She shouldn't have been surprised, but the reality of hearing Vespra's voice inches away from her was haunting.

The sound of metal dropping on the table seemed to confirm Vespra's question. "And they're enchanted, yes?"

"Of course I did," Balis answered with a tone of offense. "Your last purchase still works, doesn't it?"

"It does," Vespra said.

"Who's your next keepsake?"

"That's none of your concern."

"By the looks of it, you'll be a traveling orphanage before long. Madame Leatherby's going to have competition."

Neither Vespra nor Lazarus laughed at this remark.

Deirdre stopped eating the cake. James and Tasker fought silently over who could eat her third. Neither of them seemed concerned by the adults beside them.

"Now tell me about this treasure," Balis demanded. "The one in your letter."

James lifted his head. His fingers released a helping of cake between the plate and his mouth. Bracelets meant little to him, but treasure — that was a word that promised something sweeter than any amount of cake.

Tasker continued to shove fistfuls of chocolate into the pockets of his cheeks. He crammed so much that drool dripped from the corners of his lips.

"Are you certain you don't just want pollen?"

"I've heard the whispers of a forgotten treasure hoard that is worth more than a quarter-pound of Auro's pollen."

"Seeking out this treasure comes with its fair share of danger, though," Lazarus warned. "It would be better to take the pollen, in my opinion."

There was another pause. Glasses were lifted, sipped from, and returned to the table. James pushed the cake closer towards Tasker and crawled up to the space Deirdre was listening from.

"The story," Balis insisted.

"When the Sovereign families disappeared from Auroval," Lazarus began, "servants were instructed to gather the most prized jewels and keepsakes of court and hide them. On top of the Gloomy Peak, north of here, there is a spire filled with those very treasures; priceless riches that could make anyone more powerful than the dukes and duchesses of Elderland."

"Gloomy Peak?" Balis snorted. "Who in all of Riverbed and Elderland has the guts to travel past the Wylde and Wyldar?"

Deirdre forced a hand over James's mouth before he could volunteer himself and his guts.

An empty glass clunked on the table. "I want the real story, or I'm calling this a foul trade," Balis tested.

Deirdre watched as Vespra's cloak shifted over the floor. She couldn't see what the woman was doing, but her reaction brought upon a heavy silence. Even the occasional shuffling from the tavern owner stopped.

"You can find whole chests of these up in that spire. My own eyes have seen it. They're not worth much now, but they will be."

"Then why not take it all for yourselves?" Balis asked.

"There's only one treasure we want from that spire. A scepter made of silver."

"Why didn't you take it when you were there?"

"Couldn't touch it," Vespra said simply.

"An enchantment?" Balis smiled. "Are you paying me with a story or offering me a job?"

"That is for you to decide."

"How much would one pay for this scepter?"

Vespra rose from her seat, evidently concluding the conversation. "If you bring it to me. I'll tell you."

Balis laughed just as Tasker choked on the last piece of chocolate cake. Deirdre and James scooted back from the edge of the tablecloth, but James's sword scraped along the floor. Vespra's boots pointed in their direction.

At that moment the tavern door opened. "Frank, have you seen my son?" asked Mr. Raef.

"The cake thief?" The tavern owner chuckled. "Can't say I have. Billson has already stopped by. Poor George."

"He's calmed down. Piera offered to hollow the deelights for him so that he had time to bake another." Mr. Raef paused to make gestures of greeting towards the traders. "If any of you see three kids running around with a chocolate cake, bring them to me."

Tasker gulped uncomfortably.

Once Mr. Raef had left the tavern, Balis cleared his throat and asked, "Where will I find you, provided I get this scepter?"

"We'll find you," Vespra said.

For several minutes Deirdre, James, and Tasker sat huddled together beneath the table. They didn't dare move. After hearing the stern tone of Mr. Raef's voice, Deirdre began to feel sorry not only for herself but also for Tasker. She knew she and James could simply run away, and all punishments would disappear. Mr. and Mrs. Heart had always been fair with their punishments, but after seeing Mrs. Raef and her wooden spoon at breakfast, Deirdre feared the worst for her new friend.

At last, Frank the bartender was called out of his tavern to help roll barrels of ale towards the town square. He asked the Wayfarers to leave.

James, Tasker, and Deirdre ditched the cake plate beneath the table and scurried back out into the alleyway. There was a tub of collected rainwater, which they used to wash their hands, arms, and faces. Each member of the heist took turns inspecting another's fingernails and teeth. When they were certain that no evidence of chocolate cake remained, they strolled out of the alley and took the longest route home. The further from the bakery, the better.

"Grounded!" Mrs. Raef said heatedly as they entered the house. "All of you. Grounded."

"For what?" Tasker asked as stupidly as he could.

"Stealing from Billson and George Bartyseed!"

"We didn't steal anything," James answered back with such believable exasperation that Deirdre almost believed him herself.

"Oh no?" There wasn't a hint of trust from Mrs. Raef as she glowered at her son. "Billson said he saw you lurking outside the shop, and he clearly described you, Miss Deirdre."

"I wasn't lurking. I was showing Deirdre the shop," Tasker shouted defensively.

Mrs. Raef was red in the face. Her right hand reached for a wooden spoon. "Don't raise your voice at me, young man, and don't you dare lie."

"I'm not lying. I showed Deirdre the bakery. She helped Mr. Billson in, and then we left."

"Was that before James started creating a fiasco in the kitchen?"

Deirdre couldn't help but look towards James. She was dumbfounded at how quickly he and Tasker were fabricating a story. They hadn't discussed or rehearsed anything. "I wasn't in the kitchen."

Mrs. Raef pulled the wooden spoon from the counter. "Billson gave a perfectly accurate description of you too. If you weren't there, why would he give your description?"

"James was playing tag with Ena, Kurt, and Avee," Tasker interrupted.

"Tag?" Mrs. Raef repeated. Her stiff tone had eased slightly. Apparently, Billson had shared the detail of seeing other kids playing this game.

"Yeah, Tag." Tasker stretched his arm out and gave James a light shove as if to show how the game worked. This was his fatal mistake. Deirdre, James, and Tasker had failed to check under their sleeves for chocolate.

"Liar," hissed Mrs. Raef. Her eyes turned wild with motherly rage as she spotted a glob of chocolate on her son's upper forearm. "Tasker Beatrice Raef!" she screamed with such ferocity that all three children jumped. "What have I told you about lying?!" she advanced on him.

Deirdre wanted Tasker to run and hide, to do anything to avoid the scolding that marched towards him. But Mrs. Raef's anger had petrified them all in place. Tasker yelped as the spoon swatted his extended arm. He recoiled and found the courage to run.

"Don't you dare turn away from me!" she shrieked. Marching past James and Deirdre, she chased her son towards the stairs. The woman reached deep into her pollen pouch and called for a fistful to weigh her son's feet to the floor. Mrs. Raef caught up to him at the top of the stairs. *Whack!* The spoon hit Tasker's buttocks. "Don't you ever lie to your mother!" Tasker tried to get into his room. "Don't you ever steal again!"

Tasker wailed.

Whack!

"You think this is bad? Wait until your father finds out!"

James tugged Deirdre by the arm. "Run," he whispered.

"What about —"

"He's a goner," James said morbidly.

The spoon broke, but that didn't stop Mrs. Raef from setting her son straight. Deirdre and James slipped out the door as Tasker screamed apologies over and over again.

-IVX-

THE HARVESTING FESTIVAL

Back around the perimeter of town, James led Deirdre back towards the docks. It wasn't until they had stepped onto the old wooden planks that Deirdre finally realized where they were. "We aren't leaving now, are we?"

"Venture into the night and miss the Harvesting Festival?" James scoffed. He picked up their rolls of mellomoss. "Nah, tomorrow we'll go."

Deirdre didn't ask him if "going" meant home or towards the Gloomy Peak. She could see the gleam in his eyes. It was the same look that kept pulling her away from the comfort of her home and closer towards grumpaguls, wizzes, and wooden spoons.

James and Deirdre walked over a narrow stone bridge, which joined the town of Mill Pond with the island where the rickety, old mill stood. James pulled on a cast-iron handle and opened the wooden door with ease. "We can sleep in here tonight."

Deirdre frowned as she caught sight of several cobwebs. "Why can't we stay at the Raefs' house?"

"Tasker and Mr. Raef snore like frost bulls. You wouldn't sleep a wink with their hog-like roars. Trust me. If you want to dream, here is where you'll want to be, and are you even sure you want to go back there right now?"

Deirdre grimaced. "But it's dark in here. I can't see a thing."

James dropped the mellomoss and sighed. "Gimme a little time."

Standing in the dark, Deirdre watched James wave his hands around in circles. Silver pollen appeared in a luminescent haze. It pulsed brighter as it grew. James grabbed a handful of the cloud he had called and tossed it into the room.

"Well, don't just stand there!" he said reproachfully.

Deirdre reached out delicately. She had never held pollen before; her parents had been strict about not touching their pollen when they called. Pup had broken this rule a few times, and he was scorned for it. Despite her immense curiosity, Deirdre's hand hovered over the silver mist.

"Go on," James insisted.

The pollen felt like warm foam. There was barely any density to it. Deirdre could feel bits of the silvery cloud seep between her fingers. "What do I do with it?"

James took his third handful. "You just take it," he explained simply. With a long and exaggerated gesture, he swung his arm up and released the little cloud. Light began to stretch around the room.

Deirdre followed his exact instructions and gestures, but the pollen landed on the ground with a flop. "What did I do wrong?"

"Nothing. You just imagined it on the ground and not in the air."

"Imagined?"

"Well, that's the basic rule of calling. Imagine what you want, and that's what the pollen will do." He slapped another handful of silver mist into Deirdre's hands. "Look around the room and find a shadowed corner."

"What about the special words?"

James raised an eyebrow. "Raw pollen only hears your thoughts."

Deirdre looked at the broken rafters above her head and at the coat of dust below her feet. Old lanterns hung from the few hooks, but none of them contained candles. In the faint shadows, Deirdre could see rusted gears that had perhaps once turned but now sat disengaged. Something in the rafters moved. It slunk across gradients of shadows. A tail was raised high as it flicked back and forth. Deirdre tried to get a better look.

"See a spot?" James asked while he wiped dust off of the fallen orb of pollen.

"I think so."

"Don't think," James discouraged. "Imagine."

Deirdre stared at a far-off nook where the shadowed creature had gone. She pictured the light in her hand hovering in that area like the other messy bulb-shaped clouds above her. Holding her breath, Deirdre swung her arm and released the cloud. It wobbled between the open space and the ground for a moment, but she didn't watch it. Her eyes remained fixed on the dark spot in the room. Slowly, the pollen traveled. She blinked in disbelief.

"You're a natural!"

Deirdre beamed with pride.

"Do it again!"

Deirdre, now with more confidence, grabbed a fistful of pollen.

"Where?"

"Anywhere!"

She looked around the room, having already forgotten about the creature lurking in the shadows. There was more than enough light already. No real shadows remained. The cloud began to feel like partially melted cookie dough in her hand. Then a smirk formed out of Deirdre's thoughts. She turned and threw the handful of pollen at James.

Poof! The silver mist burst open upon impact and rained specks of glittering light around his head. James stumbled back in surprise and laughter. "What was that for?"

"You said anywhere." Deirdre grinned.

James grabbed a handful for retaliation.

Deirdre jumped out of the way but felt the remnants burst against a rusted gear behind her. She reached out to grab from the main cloud, but James whistled, and it moved away from her. "Nuh-uh!" he teased.

Deirdre took cover as James called for a larger orb of pollen. Then he made a throwing motion, and Deirdre ducked behind her stack of crates. Nothing happened. Deirdre peered back. James stood proudly with a devious grin. His eyes twitched to a spot above her. She followed his gaze. A blinding light of glowing pollen dropped on her like a bucket of water. Glitter and silver smoke billowed out around her and across the floor. She could hear James howling with laughter, and when she finally looked towards him, he was clutching his stomach and pointing at her.

"That wasn't fair," Deirdre declared, though she too was laughing.

"That was me winning," James jeered.

When he finally collected himself, he nodded towards the door. "Let's go," he said.

Deirdre attempted to pat bits of glitter off her dress. Although she couldn't get rid of them all, she realized the speckled dusting made the fabric sparkle like her windstone. Walking out into the final moments of daylight, James grabbed Deirdre by the hand.

"What?" she asked uncomfortably.

"Watch," James said with a sincere tone, which he had not yet used around her. He gestured out towards the pond that lay before them. As the sun dipped below the horizon, dark water spread like black ink dripped in a well of blue. Deirdre watched the pond turn dark all the way to its edges. James whirled his finger, directing her attention to the silhouette of Mill Pond. They waited a moment longer, standing on the center of the bridge, listening to the water ripple away, and then the town square brightened. Deirdre couldn't see what had caused it at first, but then, one by one, a series of glowing balloon-like objects began to rise.

"What are those?" Deirdre whispered in awe.

"Those are deelights," James said before giving her hand a gentle tug. "They're a type of squash that only grows in the Harvesting Hills. They taste gross, but the shells are paper-thin. People spend all day hollowing the squashes out and letting them dry. Then, at sundown, everyone lights little candles inside them."

Deirdre kept her eyes trained on the dozens of deelights now hovering over Mill Pond.

Music started playing in the streets. Cheering arose shortly after, followed by clapping, singing, and the indisputable sigh of people dancing. The celebration of a successful harvest had begun.

James rushed Deirdre through the streets and into the town square where everyone was gathered. There were tables set up for people to sit around and tables set up for people to dance on, but the tables James was most excited to get to were set up with a multitude of delicious foods.

"Look, Deirdre!" James hooted with uncontrollable bliss. "They have red berry pies, carrot cake stew, barrels of pumpkin-apple cider, and the little flakey bread rolls." James had to hold onto the edge of the table because his legs were caught in an uncontrolled jig. "Another chocolate cake!"

"Keep away from it," snapped George Bartyseed.

Deirdre's eyes fell to the ground.

"Oh, come now, George," Billson chimed. "They're just kids."

"Thieves."

"Kids."

George frowned at James for a moment more, but then his eyes relaxed and his cheeks rose. "Don't go hogging all of it this time," he said while offering a piece to Deirdre. She looked up and smiled feebly.

"What do you think of the festival?" Billson asked her.

"It's amazing, and all of it was set up so fast," Deirdre answered. It took her hours by herself just to set up her room for a tea party.

"Anything can be done on time if everyone helps," Mrs. Raef said as she appeared from behind a serving table without her wooden spoon. She seemed pleased to see them.

"Hello," Deirdre said sheepishly.

"Hi, mum!" James said happily.

She passed them two plates full of vegetables. "I saw you two running on over. I'm surprised you're even hungry."

"When am I not?" James replied.

George snorted back a laugh.

"Tasker is over there," Mrs. Raef told him before ushering them along.

"How many hits of the spoon did you end up getting?" James called out as he and Deirdre approached Tasker.

"A lot," Tasker said. He rubbed his rear end. "But I'd say secretly that it was worth it."

"So, you're not grounded?"

"Not yet," Tasker said wearily. He looked towards his father, who was encircled by a group of farmers.

"Deirdre and I are leaving to go find treasure tomorrow. You're coming, right?" James asked.

Up until this point, Deirdre hadn't thought to say anything. She hadn't received a bullying look from Tasker since the early afternoon, which led her to think he was finally accepting her as a friend. This was a victory, indeed. At the mention of treasure, however, Deirdre considered reminding James that she still needed to get home.

Tasker dropped his fork and his eyes widened. "Through the Wylde and Wyldar Woods?" He gasped as if the places he had named should not have been spoken out loud.

"To the Gloomy Peak," James added.

"You're crazy!" Tasker croaked. "You're sugar-brained. Tell me you're joking."

James's devious smile, which he wore all too well, returned in reply. "I'm not joking. You aren't afraid to go, are you, Tasker Beatrice Raef?"

Tasker gulped. "Don't say my middle name. You know how scary the edge of the Wylde Wood is…"

"And you know I've found a secret path that cuts through it, Beatrice."

"I heard those people. A treasure that can only be seen and not touched? What are we going to do with that? Look at it and go home?"

"There's plenty more treasure than that."

Deirdre tried to focus on their conversation, but there was so much more to give her attention to. The Harvesting Festival was wonderful to watch. There was so much happiness and dancing to take part in. Those who were moving to the music swung wildly about — swapping partners, spinning beneath outstretched arms, and splashing water from the fountain as they passed it.

Deirdre had never seen such a festive occasion. Part of her wished her parents were with her. She knew they would have been amongst the many dancers. Mr. Heart had two goofy feet, or at least that is what Mrs. Heart always said. She, on the other hand, was a wonderful dancer. On several occasions, Deirdre had spotted her mother trotting through the house to music in her own head.

"Do you want to dance?" Deirdre interrupted.

"What?" James replied as he was drawn out of his conversation.

Tasker, who had been waiting for any excuse to stop talking about dangerous treasures, scooted off of his chair and scurried towards the dessert tent.

"Do you want to dance with me?" Deirdre repeated. She extended a hand towards James. She had never had proper lessons herself, but she wanted to join the frivolity.

For the first time, James failed to exert any confidence. He stammered and mumbled a string of incomprehensible words before Deirdre laughed and tugged him away from the table.

"Come on!" she said, pulling him into the spiraling madness.

It didn't take long for Deirdre to learn that she didn't need to know how to dance. Each person had their own unique motions — whether graceful, goofy, or grand. Some twirled while others glided from side to side and step to step. It was as if each dancer threaded themselves through the crowd to create a dancing quilt above the cobblestone.

Deirdre could not stop laughing. James was by no means a graceful dancer. He flailed, wiggled, and rolled in all directions. His face scrunched itself into dozens of silly expressions while he flapped his arms like a squat bird. Sometimes Deirdre would be pulled into his arms for a moment, and he'd make her copy his motions, and other times he pushed her into the sea of people to dance among them on her own. The night continued…

When the deelights finally started to peak in their ascent, a single trumpet wailed to quiet the band and halt the dancing mob. A wooden chair was ceremoniously placed on the edge of the fountain. The whole town gathered before it.

"What's going on?" Deirdre whispered. The town had fallen into quiet reverence.

"Listen," James whispered. His eyes were fixed on the chair. "Just wait and listen."

-VX-

THE NIGHT OF ABSENTIA

Deirdre waited. She waited, and she listened, and she craned her neck as the townsfolk gathered. A violinist played an eerie tune as the last of the people situated themselves. But then she heard the dull thunk of wood against stone. She twisted around as it grew steadily louder and closer to the fountain.

"There he is," Tasker said as he peered over the shoulders of two people in front of them.

"Who?" Deirdre asked anxiously. She wished someone had warned her that this was a part of the festival.

"Mr. Averwood," James whispered.

Deirdre shifted around in her cramped space, trying to make herself more comfortable. When the effort proved useless, she wrapped her arms around her knees and watched the chair resting on the fountain. Mr. Averwood, the town's librarian, stepped up to the chair. His shepherd's cane was clutched in both hands. Gold trimmings curled around it, and a celebratory bow hung just beneath the curve. It took Mr. Averwood time to find his way onto the seat, but as he situated himself, he smiled pleasantly towards the crowd as if he could see them.

"Look," Deirdre whispered to James. On the far edge of the town's square, a few colorfully cloaked people gathered. They were equally observant of Mr. Averwood, but they were most definitely not a part of the town.

"What are they still doing here?" James asked as he recognized the Wayfarers from earlier that day.

Mr. Averwood cleared his throat. The violinist's instrument fell silent. Then with a loud crack from his shepherd's cane, the librarian called upon a great cloud of white pollen. It unraveled and webbed out from the base of his cane before collecting above him.

"Even as we celebrate the present," Mr. Averwood said firmly, "it is important that we remember our past." The pollen above him twisted and turned like a bottled storm. "We gather here tonight because of another successful harvest."

A few cheers responded from the crowd.

"And with each successful year, it is important to remember that the younger are getting wiser, and we old farmers are getting more stubborn."

The audience chuckled, and for a split second, Deirdre felt as though Mr. Averwood had looked directly at her, Tasker, and James.

"With our world ever-changing, it is my responsibility to remind us of how the world once was." Mr. Averwood took another long pause and then began. "It has been ten years since Riverbed claimed its independence from Elderland. Ten years since we were governed by the High Sovereigns of Auroval."

Deirdre watched as his pollen cloud took the shape of a great city; the same one she'd seen from the River Olde.

"And in those ten years, the moons have continued to rise and fall." Three little orbs of light arched slowly over the cloud city. "We've shoveled through the snowy seasons of Frostforth, just as we have tilled soil through the hot seasons of Heatspell. We've done it all, together."

Heads in the crowd bowed in agreement.

"And that is because ten years ago, on one particular night of Absentia, the thrones of our former Sovereigns were challenged by a madman whose name was Malgarath."

Deirdre looked at James and Tasker. Both of them seemed to know this person Mr. Averwood spoke of.

"As the founding principles of Elderland commanded, there was always supposed to be four sovereigns. Two were appointed by the eldestree, Auro. And two were chosen by the people of our realm. Together the Sovereigns ensured all of Elderland thrived, and for many generations it did. We all followed *One Law*, an idea that pollen could be called upon by anyone at any age so long as they did not harm another person or eldestree."

"Until the ceaseless tide turns," the crowd replied solemnly. James and Tasker said these words too. Deirdre had heard her father say this phrase in passing before, but it had always been silly words to her, like when Mr. Heart declared that something "smelled like pine." Hearing an entire town echo a phrase about ceaseless tides awoke her curiosity.

Mr. Averwood continued, "Some people used pollen to further our understanding of Calling, but there were those who manipulated it for only their personal gain. Mordryll came into existence — a weaponized form of pollen. And Malgarath, the self-proclaimed First Hand of Mordryll, demanded that he should be given a fifth seat among the Sovereign thrones. But he was denied…"

Deirdre was unsettled by the sounds of adults crying. Younger children around her listened in fear. It became evident to Deirdre that they all knew this story; this history of Elderland that she had not been taught.

Mr. Averwood wore the same expression Deirdre's father did when retelling a harrowing tale. And whatever details the librarian saw, his cloud of pollen above him shared it.

"… ten years ago, on a night of Absentia, where none of our moons illuminate the sky, Malgarath used his power to lay siege on the city of Auroval. The First Hand and his legion broke through the city's walls and charged up towards the castle, destroying everything in their path."

Spires in the cloud city above Mr. Averwood exploded and crumbled. The pollen writhed in flames as it tore itself apart.

"But the High Sovereigns were prepared," Mr. Averwood said. "They sealed the doors to their own throne room with enchantments. Malgarath's war ended as swiftly as it had begun. He and his followers were stripped of their power, and the practice of Mordryll hasn't been witnessed since."

Deirdre watched the pollen cloud settle. The whole town mourned quietly together. Mr. Averwood even cried though he kept his composure.

"Our Sovereigns saved us by abandoning us. They spared us from a worse fate, by leaving us in the ruins of *One Law*. The dukes and duchesses surrounding Auroval lifted their neighboring villages, but our towns of the west were left to our own devices. It was then that Riverbed united and formed our *Laws of Three*. Children are not permitted to call. Pollen is primarily a currency. And without the sanction of a town leader, all Calling is to be done within the privacy of one's own home. And how fortunate we all are that ten years ago, Jerald Raef was elected as the Mayor of Mill Pond!"

Deirdre looked at Tasker, who was beaming with pride as his father rose slightly from his seat to wave.

"Our years of farming with pollen are over. Our process is slower, our backs ache a little more, and there is more we have yet to learn… but that hasn't stopped our town from being great. Tonight, we celebrate that first pollen-free harvest in conjunction with this year's harvest — the largest harvest we've ever seen!"

The town gave a unanimous cheer.

"Praise be to each of you. Praise be to our Mayor. And Praise be to the Sovereigns. May the Black Star never fall!" Mr. Averwood concluded.

"May the Black Star never fall!" the town replied. Everyone stood with applause, except for Deirdre, who felt her stomach knot.

Music from the band started up once more, and people moved eagerly to dance. Before Deirdre could decide what to do, James and

Tasker dashed off without her.

Deirdre's curiosity boiled at the mention of a "Black Star." Two words had never haunted her more. She decided to talk to Mr. Averwood herself. Finding a chair, she quickly stood on it to spot the librarian.

"The pigs are eating," Mr. Raef called towards her.

Deirdre watched as the Mayor strolled towards her.

"They're getting more chocolate cake, not that they deserve it."

Mrs. Raef then appeared beside her husband. She had danced her way merrily through the crowd, laughing and accepting earnest-given gratitude for her own deeds as the Mayor's wife. Her bun had come slightly undone, and her apron was askew. "Did my boys forget you?" she asked as Mr. Raef took her hand.

"I was looking for Mr. Averwood," Deirdre replied. She steadied herself on the chair, which was balanced unevenly on the cobblestones.

"What for?" Mr. Raef asked.

Deirdre shrugged. "I had a question."

"Questions about what, dear?" Mrs. Raef persisted.

Deirdre felt uncomfortable by their firm looks. She knew they were anticipating her answer as adults typically do around sensitive topics. Feeling as though their answers would be more than three-quarters truthful, she decided to tell them her questions honestly. "What's the Black Star, what is Mordryll, where is Malgarath now, and why was everyone so upset about Auroval?"

"Don't you pay any mind to that. It's in the past now," Mrs. Raef answered quickly.

"Now, Ellie. I think she deserves a better answer than that," Mr. Raef argued.

"Those are answers her parents should give her, not us."

Deirdre hated being talked over, especially while standing at practically eye-level with them from atop her chair.

"I'll say this," Mr. Raef said. "Malgarath is gone, and he's not coming back. A common theory is that the enchantment on the doors to the Sovereign's throne room captured Malgarath's powers and bottled them up in a star."

"What we're saying is that you have nothing to worry about," Mrs. Raef added.

"But what if the Black Star falls?" Deirdre asked.

"It won't," Mrs. Raef said. "No one really even knows if there is even really a Black Star."

"And if it's any help, Tasker only hears about the Night of Absentia through Mr. Averwood's retelling, just like you. When you are all of age, I'm sure it will be taught in school. There's no need to go chasing history on your own," Mr. Raef said gently.

Deirdre accepted their answers. It wasn't what she wanted to hear, and it didn't make any more sense, but now she knew the Black Star and this madman were connected. It explained why her own parents were so shaken with fear when Vespra had said it *would* fall. She could feel the Raefs watching her with parental concern.

"I didn't know you were the Mayor of Mill Pond," she said to help end their worries.

Mr. Raef chuckled. "I didn't know you were a cake thief. Tasker said it was you who actually stole it."

Deirdre tried to contain her smile; the way Mr. Raef had spoken about it, made it sound like a compliment.

"I won't do it again," Deirdre said.

"Smart girl," Mrs. Raef said. "Are you enjoying the Harvesting Festival?" she then asked.

"I've never seen anything like it."

"Bellebrook doesn't celebrate the Crystal Moon of Autumn?"

Deirdre shook her head. "We celebrate the spring."

"An influence of your neighbors in Merrivyne, no doubt," Mr. Raef joked.

Deirdre didn't understand his remark, but she smiled and nodded politely all the same. Bellebrook's celebration was not as fun or festive as Mill Pond's autumn celebration. The streets were decorated in flower petals, and a parade of music snaked through at midday. A town-wide picnic took place in the evening, but everyone kept to their own yards. There was no real dancing or sharing of meals.

"You'll have to bring your parents next year," Mrs. Raef said to Deirdre.

This made Deirdre grin. "They'll love it," she said confidently.

It wasn't until much later that the town musicians finally started to leave for their own beds. One sleepy fiddler remained as the stars overhead gathered in the east. The strings faded to soft songs as more and more people retired for the night. Mr. and Mrs. Raef chose to depart without their son, who had collapsed face-down in his eighth slice of cake.

"Ready to go?" James asked Deirdre quietly as they observed a swaying couple. Deirdre nodded. Most of the glowing orange deelights struggled to hover above the ground; a few had even sunk as low as Deirdre's waist as she and James shuffled out of the town square. When they neared the edge of the festival, a goofy smirk appeared on James's face. "You know what my favorite part about this festival is?"

"What?" Deirdre asked.

"This."

James gestured towards the lingering people — dancing, dining, or sleeping in the square. One by one the candles inside the squashes were extinguished by the wind. The deelights dropped out of the sky and splattered the stragglers. The fiddler, who had foreseen this, was tucked away beneath the awning over Piera Petal's flower shop. James and Deirdre snickered as delirious people jolted awake and laughed at themselves for being covered in pulpish goo.

-XVI-

WYLDE AND WYLDAR WOODS

Morning arrived with golden rays of light. They were warm, but the breeze of autumn still nipped as it pushed between the boards of the mill. James reclined against a vertical post in the rafters, tinkering with a bulb of pollen. He poked and prodded it as if it were a gelatinous substance. Every so often he peered down at Deirdre, who was still fast asleep. His fingers sculpted the pollen into different shapes and prisms. There wasn't any reason for it; he was simply bored of waiting. After successfully battling grumpaguls and stealing a delicious cake, James felt as though he couldn't end his adventure with Deirdre so immediately.

Yet, despite his yearnings, James also knew to honor his promises. He had promised to take Deirdre home to Bellebrook, which he still intended to do.

The pollen wobbled over his outstretched fingers. He tossed it up and caught it on the back of his hand. James glanced down again. Only Deirdre's yellow hair was visible beneath her blanket. She hadn't moved in hours. James concluded that she was a wonderful adventurer — arguably better than Tasker, though he'd never tell Tasker this.

A bitter feeling trickled in when he thought about bringing Deirdre back home. Her parents would never let her leave their sight again. James had seen this happen before. He and a friend would share an adventure, then when he brought them home, the parents would banish him from the house. He was, they said, "a bad influence."

Of course, Mr. and Mrs. Raef were the exceptions. They kept a careful eye on him and Tasker when they played together, but not once had either Raef parent forced James away from their home. James hoped Mr. and Mrs. Heart would be like them.

Deirdre gave a sudden stir, and James turned his attention back towards the silver mist. He directed it around the room with his eyes. It flew in between the rafters, around the iron gears, and among different barrels and crates. He made it do loops and zigzags, willing it to go faster as time crawled on.

Then he noticed something in the highest corner of the mill. Its figure was murky in the dusty haze, but James could tell with some certainty that it was a folisangel. He blocked some of the glare with a curved palm and squinted. The winged cat looked back at him. Its tail swayed rhythmically back and forth.

Clenching his fists momentarily, James called for the pollen to return to him. His hands burned slightly as the silver pollen returned to his veins. He had grown used to this discomfort. Treliave had promised him that, in time, the burning sensation would fade altogether.

With slow and deliberate movements, James stood, centering his weight on the rafters. Teetering above the floor of the mill, he crept over to the center mechanism and began to climb. He kept an eye on the folisangel, and it regarded him with the same attentiveness.

Once at eye-level, James recognized the pristine white fur and nubby, charcoal-black horns. This folisangel was named Pahlah.

James had met it during his quest to return Deirdre's missing mitten. Vespra, who had entrusted him with that task, had done so only after he had failed to steal a treasure map from her carriage.

In truth, James hadn't been entirely sure if the parchment he had seen had been a treasure map, but it had looked like one. The page was yellow with age. A map of Riverbed and Elderland was drawn on it in ink, and there was a spot north of the Lower Sleeping Giant marked with an X.

"She goes wherever I cannot," Vespra had explained to James after she had caught him by the wrist. "Her eyes are my eyes, her ears are my ears, so don't do anything foolish now."

James inched closer with an outstretched hand and waited for Pahlah to move closer. When it flicked its tail, he shifted onto the same wooden beam as it. James mirrored Pahlah's stance. The tail stopped swaying, and Pahlah chirped. She blinked at him slowly and approached. Tied to her back with a red ribbon was a little note with James's name scribbled across the edge.

"James?" Deirdre called from the ground below. She sat up and rubbed her eyes before scanning the rafters. He was no longer where he had been. "James?" she called again.

Thumping and scraping echoed abruptly as her high-spirited friend came swinging down from the shadows above. "Good morning," James shouted. One hand was stuffing paper into his back pocket as the other gripped the wood beam above Deirdre. He hung there, swaying limply.

Still peering at him through sleep-squinting eyes, Deirdre asked, "What were you doing up there?" Her feet kicked the scratchy blanket away.

James waved his dangling hand, and his wooden sword came rushing towards him. He caught it before giving it a hefty swing. "I was preparing for another adventure," he roared.

Deirdre covered her ears and frowned. She was inexplicably tired. James, on the other hand, was already busying himself by fighting an army of invisible foes.

Deirdre tried running a hand through her hair. Knots. She winced as her fingers pulled through a few. "Ready?" James asked all too quickly.

"Not yet."

He snapped his fingers and the beds of mellomoss floated over to him. With great haste, he rolled them up, tied them with string, and tossed them onto a stack of crates. "How about now?"

"No." Deirdre sighed. She was now surveying her dress, which had become a frightful mess.

James rolled his eyes. "What are we waiting for?"

Deirdre looked up at him. His hair stuck out with cowlicks in all directions. There were remnants of last night's soup on his shirt and dirt everywhere else. "We're waiting for me to look presentable," she huffed. "And that's not easy to do when I've been wearing the same dress for three days." Pulling her hair into view, Deirdre tried to braid it as best as she could. Her mother usually did it for her, but Deirdre had been learning.

"Look presentable?" James scoffed. This had been the silliest thing Deirdre had ever tried to do, and yet, he had noticed she was constantly trying to do it. "We're on an adventure."

"So?"

"So stop playing with your hair. It's time to go." James pulled open the door to the mill, letting the sunlight flood in. "Today we're going to find the treasure that can be seen but not touched!"

Deirdre stopped trying to rub the stains out of her dress. "No, we're going home."

"After," James said. "This adventure won't take long."

"Yes, it will." Deirdre thought of what Treliave had shown her.

"Nah, the Gloomy Peak is practically on the way to Bellebrook." James leaned out of the mill's doorway. "I can practically see it from here," he shouted.

Deirdre arched an eyebrow. "No, it's not. It's nowhere near here or on the way."

"Sure it is."

"Bellebrook is southwest, and the Wyldar Woods are north. How does that make any sense?"

"We've already sailed east to go west," James argued.

"Yes, because I don't know how to swim. I do know how to walk."

"Not to the Wyldar Woods. You've never been there."

Deirdre stomped her foot. "Treliave showed me the Adventure Map. I know where it is."

James's jaw dropped. His cheeks flushed. "When? Where was I?"

"You had already left the treehouse," Deirdre said while she shrugged on her coat and straightened her posture. James grumbled something under his breath. "What did you say?"

"I said if you want to go home, you have to stick with me, and I'm going to find that treasure first."

Deirdre wanted to scream. She was no longer in the mood for adventures; she no longer wanted to spend time with this irritable boy. Her parents were most certainly beside themselves without her, and even though she had sent them a letter, she needed to go home now. "I don't need you. Mr. and Mrs. Raef will help me find a cart traveling to Marketfair." She folded her arms across her chest.

"They can't help you today, sleepyhead." James flashed a wry grin. "The farmers leave for Marketfair at sunrise. You'd have to wait a whole 'nother day and night."

Deirdre stood firm, trying to detect a lie.

"I'll walk there myself then," she concluded.

"You'll never make it on foot alone." James strolled, unconcerned, out the door. "Follow me on this adventure," he said over his shoulder. "And you'll be home with the rising moon."

Hardly pleased by the start of her day, Deirdre marched after James in frustration. She tugged on her mittens and said nothing more to him until later that afternoon.

Deirdre and James left Mill Pond with a knapsack of bread rolls and fruit, packed by Mrs. Raef, who also informed them that Tasker would not be joining them for their next adventure. He was bedridden with a stomach ache. It was a believable story, but when Tasker failed to show himself to say goodbye, Deirdre wondered if Tasker had asked his mother to lie about his sickness. She recalled how frightened he had been at the thought of traveling to the Wylde Woods.

Deirdre refused to speak to James as he led them west along the edge of the River Olde. She had not forgotten how rude he had been to her at the start of their morning. But despite her feelings towards him, Deirdre recognized that it was another good day to travel. The sun was out with only wisps of white clouds, and the morning autumn wind had settled. Fallen leaves were everywhere, rustling and crinkling as Deirdre walked on them.

When they reached a narrow, back-flowing creek, James followed it without comment. What had started as a spacious walk on wild grass along the riverbank, now turned into a muddy hike. Deirdre was forced to walk in James's wake. She took this time to make faces at him behind his back to disperse her frustrations with him.

The creek tumbled north into a forest where the trees grew tightly beside one another. Their roots were knotted and tangled above the ground. Ivy and moss-covered vines draped from branches like thick green snakes. They reminded Deirdre of Mrs. Doris's knitted scarf.

"Are these the Wylde Woods?" she asked as they moved cautiously along the forest's edge. Her right hand instinctively squeezed her pocketed windstone.

"Yes," James whispered. He rummaged inside their knapsack and passed her a bread roll.

"How far until we reach the Wyldar Woods?" Deirdre was starting to doubt James would have her home by nightfall.

"Not far," James said. "We just have to walk through there." He pointed towards the ivy-tangled trees. The sunlight dimmed as it battled through the thick canopy of purple leaves.

"Why don't we just cut through it now?"

"It's better to stay near the water for now," James stated hastily.

Deirdre lifted an eyebrow. "Are you afraid to go in there?"

"No," James answered sharply. "I'm the bravest, remember?" He hoisted the knapsack higher onto his shoulder and patted his wooden sword. "Nothing scares me."

"Then why not go into the woods?"

"Because there are wrestling roots and snarling saplings that would try to eat us. I know a secret path that's protected. It'll take us straight to the Wyldar Woods."

"What are wrestling roots and snarling saplings?"

"They're the trees of the Wylde Woods. They grow from sour soil, so their roots spread over the surface of the ground instead of deep into the dirt. To sweeten it, they wrestle wanderers and bury them alive."

Deirdre glanced towards the trees. "That's horrible."

"And snarling saplings are the youngest Wylde Wood trees. You'll hear them pass messages to the older trees when travelers enter."

Trying to think of ways to outsmart the Wylde Woods, Deirdre said, "I wish we had brought your moonstone; then we could float over the forest."

James shook his head. "Too easy."

"Too easy, what's wrong with too easy?"

"No," James explained. "Too easy for them." James nodded towards the curled trunks and woven walls of branches. "These trees are taller than they seem. When something flies above the forest, they unfurl and snatch whatever tries to pass over them. The vertical vines, which wrap around their trunks, are extensions to their reach as well. The trees fling them up like nets. That's why birds fly around the forest and not over."

"Why doesn't anyone sweeten the soil?" Deirdre wondered out loud, thinking that pollen must be a simple remedy.

"As terrible as the Wylde Woods are, they're the only barrier that can contain the Wyldar Woods."

Deirdre shivered when James said this. A part of her didn't want to know about the Wyldar Woods now that she had reasons to fear the Wylde.

James scooped up a handful of pebbles and tossed a few into the Wylde Woods. A high-pitched wail echoed from the forest's depths. Roots that had been barely visible leapt off the ground and caught the pebbles in mid-air. The old bark twitched and growled as the roots took their prey back down into the earth to eat.

"Treliave once told me that the Wylde and Wyldar Woods used to be the most beautiful forest. The tree leaves were once sapphire blue, and their bark used to shimmer with specks of silver," James said. Deirdre followed his steps more closely. "Now they shriek, but supposedly they used to sing the most beautiful melodies."

"I wonder if they were eldestrees."

"If they were, they became evil," James told her. "Treliave warned me when I adventured to its edge that Wyldar Woods created monstrous shadow creatures."

"Like grumpaguls?"

"Worse than grumpaguls." James tossed more pebbles into the woods and tried to see how deep into the tree line he could get them before they were eaten by roots. This had been one of the first games he had ever created. In his head, James counted down the seconds before the saplings screamed. He then took notice of Deirdre's looks of fear.

"Don't worry. We'll be safe. Shadow monsters can only travel in shadows."

"Did you come across one when you adventured to the Wyldar Woods?"

"Nope," James said cheerfully. "I found the secret path that leads to its edge, picked up the black rock, and ran away as fast as I could."

Deirdre's feet sank into the mud as she watched the wrestling roots fight over the pebbles. "Have you ever seen the Gloomy Peak?"

"I've seen it from Treliave but not up close."

"Why is it called the Gloomy Peak?" Deirdre was hoping for a story less frightful than the history of the Wylde and Wyldar Woods.

"It's called Gloomy Peak because of the dark cloud hanging above it. I heard once that it's the only dark cloud in the whole world. It never moves. It never rains. It just floats there, as if too sad to drift away."

Deirdre continued to eye the Wylde Woods warily. She imagined the roots slithering out beyond their limits with the intent of dragging her into the gloom. Perhaps Tasker had been wise to eat too much cake. This was much too dangerous for someone her age.

"Found it!" James sang. He scooped up another handful of stones from the creek and tossed them between two specific trees whose trunks bore strange carvings. Although the roots wriggled and writhed, they never left the forest floor. The scattered stones remained untouched, teasing the wild trees.

Snarling Saplings sounded as James entered the forest. Their ear-splitting screeches raised hairs on the back of Deirdre's neck, but none of the roots attacked. Nevertheless, Deirdre remained skeptical as she inched closer to the Wylde Woods. With each step, her breath drew tighter. She practically suffocated herself without the help of the Wylde, until she took James's hand and crossed into the forest.

The Saplings shrieked furiously. Deirdre closed her eyes and pressed her hands firmly over her ears. She froze. She refused to move. Tears welled up despite her attempts to stay brave. This was all wrong. This was not an adventure; it was a nightmare. She wanted to go home. She wanted her parents.

Then, carefully, James took one of Deirdre's hands into his own.

"Stick with me. I'll keep you safe," he reassured her. The shrieking had stopped. Distant roots still groped and snapped at them, but each attempt failed.

Deirdre fought the urge to run back to the River Olde. She met James's eyes and stared into them. He held her gaze while slowly drawing his wooden sword. Then he placed the hilt into her hand.

"If anything comes too close to you, take a good swing at it, and it won't bother you again."

"Promise?" Deirdre quivered.

"No time for breaking promises," James replied with a wink.

None of this calmed Deirdre completely, but it encouraged her enough to move forward. She followed James deeper into the woods. He led the way for what seemed like forever. The air smelled of wet moss. Occasionally, a root would bend around its trunk, desperate to lick even the slightest bit of the wandering children. Deirdre would yelp in fright and anger before slashing the tip of the root. She found the dull wood somehow cut with as much precision as a sharpened metal blade.

As James and Deirdre approached the end of the path, the gnarled trees of the Wylde slowly stood rigid like guards before a gateway. In the folds of their ancient bark, Deirdre spied small specks of silver. The remnants of the Wylde's past glittered weakly out to her, and beyond them new darkness presented itself. It was like a thick curtain had been dropped between the Wylde and Wyldar; a distinct divide that neither could cross. James came to a halt.

The Wylde's floor of great overgrowth stopped where the Wyldar's exposed black, cracked stone began. Sunlight failed to illuminate the Wyldar through its heavy gray leaves. Nothing seemed to grow within. It was a vacant cavern of scorched earth and dead columns of wood.

"Now what?" Deirdre whispered. Surely the shadow monsters were lurking just out of sight. She felt for the windstone in her pocket.

"I'm not sure," James said. "We need light to cross safely. Enough to keep the shadows away."

"What about pollen?"

"I don't think that's a good idea," James answered.

"Why not?"

James shrugged. "My gut told me not to."

Deirdre's gut told her to vomit up her bread roll and run the opposite way, but she was choosing to ignore it. "We could go back," she suggested feebly.

"We're almost there."

Deirdre knew "almost" was a lie, and she was about to argue that they weren't prepared enough to continue when something small moved along the edge of the darkness.

"What's that?" she said with a sharp intake of breath.

"I'm not sure," James replied curiously. He reached into the knapsack and pulled out a handful of berries.

"You're going to feed it?" Deirdre remarked skeptically. Food would surely bring it closer to them, and closer was not the direction she wanted any shadow monster to come.

James knelt at the edge of the Wyldar Woods, staying out of the reach of wrestling roots. "What shadow monster bobs up and down?" he questioned before rolling the berries onto the black earth.

Deirdre squinted, trying to gauge the full size of the monster. It seemed too small to be vicious, but then again, the grumpaguls hadn't been big when they had first flopped out of Mrs. Doris's mouth.

"Deirdre?" James whispered, holding an apple in his hand.

"What?"

"Can you pass me my sword?"

"No," Deirdre replied as she gripped the sword tighter.

James didn't ask her for it again. Instead, he bit a large chunk out of the apple and tossed it towards the scattered berries.

"Why are we trying to feed it?" Deirdre hissed.

"What shadow monster eats fruit?" James posed. He had never encountered one before, but if grumpaguls were shadow monsters, then they didn't eat fruit. James also considered that grumpaguls were more like shadow pests than full-grown monsters.

The creature moved forward. It bobbed up and down awkwardly as if its head was too heavy for its neck. But then Deirdre realized it didn't have a neck at all. The creature was nothing more than a ball of fuzz with big eyes and a star-tipped tail.

"A wiz!" she exclaimed through a stifled scream of relief.

Neon light expelled the shadows surrounding the wiz. The creature opened its mouth to reveal a blue-stained tongue. Deirdre recognized this particular wiz to be the one she had refused to bonk. It hiccupped excitedly at her and then hiccupped back towards the darkness. A dozen more wizzes appeared. Some of them raced for the scattered berries and apple, while others floated carefully towards Deirdre and James.

"Brilliant," James said. "Deirdre, you're brilliant!" Stepping into the Wyldar Woods, he hollered, "Wiz!" and all the floating creatures lit up the forest. "They can't live in the sunlight, so they hide where it's darkest during the day. They must use the same path we walked on to get out of here at night to find food."

Deirdre cautiously stepped across the divide between Wylde and

Wyldar Woods. It was not as scary now that they had light; it now reminded her of an empty attic. Biz gave her a gentle nuzzle under her chin.

"Hello." She giggled before giving it a soft pat on the top of its face.

"It's *click-tock*," James told her. "To say hello in Wizzish."

"You speak Wizzish?"

James made a series of hiccupping, popping, and snapping sounds. Another wiz looked at him and replied through a mouthful of apple.

"What did you say?" she asked.

"I asked for directions," James replied. "I'm quite fluent in Wizzish."

Deirdre wasn't entirely sure she believed him. Despite her doubts, James had indeed asked where the Gloomy Peak was. A moment later, the glowing wizzes formed a ring of light around them and offered to guide them through the Wyldar. Biz floated beside a much-relieved Deirdre. It popped and hiccupped at her as they walked.

"He likes you." James laughed as Biz perched itself comfortably on Deirdre's shoulder. She could feel the soft fur smush and mold around her collarbone.

"Do you know what he's saying?"

James listened to the specific gibberish that Biz emitted. "It's thanking you for not bonking it the other night and apologizing for eating the berries you picked without asking. It also hopes you didn't have another nightmare." James looked at her. "What's a nightmare?"

Deirdre was stunned that James didn't know. She tried to hide her face by looking at Biz. How did this little creature know about her nightmare? "I'm not sure," she told James. "I've never heard of a nightmare before." The lie she provided seemed to satisfy his curiosity.

"Sometimes they make up words if they don't have one for it. Wizzish only has about five hundred words in total," James explained. When Deirdre didn't ask him how he knew this, he said, "I'm going to see how much further the walk to the Gloomy Peak is."

"Here, take this," Deirdre said before passing him the sword. "I have enough protection now." She pointed carefully towards the wiz on her shoulder.

James chuckled. "Can I trade you?" he asked while extending the knapsack. Deirdre nodded and took it from him. James then stepped forward and started jabbering with one of the wizzes up ahead.

Untying a corner of the cloth that held their snacks, Deirdre rummaged for a handful of berries. She fed one to Biz. When the other wizzes detected this, they shot their companion envious looks. Deirdre opened her palm so that, one by one, they could each float over and lick up a berry. Their tiny tongues felt like strips of sandpaper. The sensation reminded Deirdre of Pup whenever he showed her affection.

Deirdre missed her kitten, and she felt guilty for not thinking about him more often. She wondered if he had been fed. It was typically her responsibility, but she assumed her mother and father wouldn't let him starve while she was away. Her parents loved Pup. Her father was always sneaking him table scraps while he cooked. And her mother spent hours at a time sitting in the living room rocking chair, pampering Pup with pets while he slept in her lap.

"Biz," peeped the wiz on Deirdre's shoulder. It rolled along her shoulder and down her arm before flopping into her open hand that was now free of berries.

Deirdre looked around to see that all the other wizzes were glowing bright with satisfaction. Biz wriggled in her hand; its soft fuzz tickled her fingers.

"Alright," she told it, recognizing it hoped to be petted. Gently stroking the top of its head with two fingers, Deirdre looked towards James, who had been very engrossed in his own conversation with a lazy-eyed wiz. "Have you asked them if they've seen the treasure we're looking for?"

"Yes," James replied. "This one says they stay away from the Gloomy Peak. Apparently, a pack of shadow hounds hunt up there."

"What are shadow hounds?"

Almost immediately the wizzes began to hiccup anxiously. Their bright eyes darted back and forth. Little pointy ears emerged from the tops of their heads. In an instant, the ring of light dispersed into the

Wyldar. The faint light of day, diluted by a gray sky, appeared in the distance. The edge of the Wyldar was nearby. Biz remained in the palm of Deirdre's hand, and a lazy-eyed wiz floated over James. Two other wizzes continued orbiting around them, attempting to fend off the darkness. Deirdre and James began hearing the low and hungry growls of monsters lurking in the surrounding shadows. They quickened their pace.

Something howled from behind them. Deirdre and James were left with three wizzes — the third one spinning around them like a comet.

"Run!" James hissed, and the two of them fled towards the clearing. If monsters lurked in shadows, James knew they'd stray from the light up ahead.

The wiz orbiting them hiccupped, sputtered, and popped until it could no longer stay alight. Deirdre watched it give up and vanish into the Wyldar. Something in the shadows howled again. She and James were seven steps away from the clearing. Deirdre dropped the knapsack and her coat in fright. Then they were five steps away. James twisted around so that he was facing the darkness behind them. At three steps away, Biz gave one final burst of light as the lazy-eyed wiz fell behind. James shoved Deirdre ahead. She let out a scream. The two of them tumbled out of the Wyldar Woods and onto a mountain of gravel and stone.

-XVII-

THE GLOOMY PEAK

"Are you alright?" James coughed. He rolled onto his back gasping for breath.

"Fine," Deirdre replied as she panted. Her hands and knees were scuffed up. Black soot was smeared across her dress, rendering it completely ruined. At the edge of the forest, Deirdre saw Biz testing the boundary of daylight.

For a moment she and James watched. "Don't. Go hide," she said between gulps of air, though she wasn't entirely sure the Wyldar was any safer than where she and James sat. Biz didn't listen. It swooped an inch out of the forest and then back in again. It did this several times, made a peep of excitement, and then dashed over to see if Deirdre and James were okay.

"That is the most loyal wiz I have ever seen," James said in amazement as he watched Deirdre catch the wiz in her hands.

"Well, I can't imagine any wiz being loyal to you when all you do is bonk them."

James shrugged.

Deirdre looked back towards the Wyldar Woods one final time.

"My jacket!" she gasped. "Oh no, and my mittens too!" But it was at the thought of her lost windstone that she began to cry. Deirdre had intended on using it the moment she had finished her adventure with James. Walking along the River Olde earlier that morning, she had thought about sending the stone to her parents. She hoped they would receive it and, within a short while, find her safely back in their arms.

"I'm sorry," James said, noticing her tears.

"It's not your fault."

"We can try to find your jacket and mittens. It can't be too deep in the woods. Where did you drop it?"

Deirdre tried to look through the menacing tree line. The chances of finding anything without a clock of wizzes seemed hopeless. The race to safety had happened so suddenly that Deirdre struggled to even recall where she had dropped her jacket. Then she remembered dropping the knapsack along with it, and another wave of tears gushed out of her. That was the second knapsack she'd left behind.

Trying to gather some sense of composure, Deirdre looked towards the mountain. It was steep and misshapen with jagged rocks piled on top of one another. It was no more inviting than anything else she had seen today, but there weren't roots trying to wrestle her, and there was enough light to see on her own. The worst part of their adventure had to be over.

"Deirdre, where did you drop them?" James repeated.

Picturing her father giving her the windstone, Deirdre felt her lower lip tremor. Biz gave a little wiggle and escaped her cradling hands. It zoomed off and back into the woods.

"Rude," James said under his breath. This was the worst time it could have abruptly abandoned her. The sight of Deirdre's tears made him uncomfortable. Adventures were not supposed to have crying, but he also understood there had to be time made for crying.

"I just need a minute," Deirdre pleaded weakly.

James nodded with a faint smile and started cleaning his sword.

"It's beautiful," Deirdre remarked to distract herself.

James passed the sword over to her. "Treliave makes me a new one for every adventure. Travelers used to spend months sleeping beneath eldestrees with the hopes of being given a sword fashioned from their wood. If granted one, they were seen as knights."

"Do you want to be a knight?"

James snorted. "I want to be the greatest adventurer that ever lived. I want to stand on every mountaintop, sail out to all three moons, and sleep on every shore."

Deirdre ran her finger over the grooves in the hilt. The pommel had an acorn-like seed embedded in the center and engraved vines curled around the cross-guard.

Deirdre ran her index finger along the center of the blade before passing it back. "That sounds wonderful."

"What do you want to be?"

"I don't know," she replied, wrapping her arms around her knees. She thought it would sound foolish to say a tea party host. And if she was really being honest with herself, she wasn't sure she even wanted to host tea parties anymore. Before James could press her for a better answer, Biz came racing out of the Wyldar Woods again. A small object was pressed between its lips.

"Whatcha got there?" James inquired just before the wiz dropped a glass-like stone in Deirdre's lap.

Letting out a dumbfounded gasp, Deirdre scooped Biz up and pressed her lips against its furry forehead. "How did you? How could you?" She looked towards James. "Please tell him I say thank you."

James made a distinct clack before asking her, "What is that?"

"It's my windstone," she told him excitedly. "If I think of my parents and breathe on it, the wind will take it to them. They'll know where we are."

"Why didn't you send that to them when we were with Treliave?"

"I…" She paused. "I…" Deirdre thought for a moment while trying to sort through all of her feelings. "I don't know." Placing Biz in her lap, Deirdre picked up the stone and blew on it gently. The stone shimmered faintly. It hovered an inch or so above her hand and then dropped lifelessly back into her palm.

"That's it?" James asked.

"No," Deirdre snapped before thinking about her parents, her home, and Pup. She blew on it a second time. The stone shimmered even weaker than the last time. It wobbled in her palm before falling still. "What's wrong with you?" she muttered to it. Desperately, she blew on it a third time. The windstone remained lifeless in her hand.

James looked up. "Maybe it needs more wind to go," he suggested.

Deirdre noticed an edge had been freshly chipped. The windstone had broken when she dropped it. "Maybe," she said half-heartedly. "Let's go."

With a refreshed thirst in his eyes, James stared up at the mountain. He focused his gaze on a colossal black tower. "That's it!" he told Deirdre.

Thunder sounded warnings neither he nor Deirdre could understand.

Biz trembled in Deirdre's hands. She looked down and realized she had never seen a wiz in the proper light. Its fur lacked any pigment, and its eyes were as blue as the Aramayus. But what surprised Deirdre was how iridescent its star-tipped tail was.

"Ready?" James asked Deirdre, brimming with newfound excitement.

"Yes," Deirdre said as she pocketed the broken windstone.

Not caring to waste more time, they began their climb. Deirdre, who had never been less prepared for anything in her life, released Biz in order to pull herself up and around the jagged boulders. Within minutes a fresh layer of dirt coated Deirdre's hands, knees, and dress.

Deirdre noticed Biz struggled to hover by her waist the higher they climbed. "Here," she told it before ripping layers off her dress.

James blinked in disbelief. She had complained about ruining her dress throughout their entire adventure, and now she was willingly mangling it.

Deirdre held open a split in the fabric to welcome Biz. Since her pockets were too small, she had contrived a different spot for it to rest. The wiz zipped inside and sighed.

After nearly an hour of climbing, James declared that they should take a short break. He scrambled up one final boulder as Deirdre plopped herself on a rocky surface below. Shadows cast by the cloud above stretched only as far as the Wyldar's edge. Much like the contrast of a pencil sketched portrait in an unfinished painting, the kingdom of Elderland's color clashed miraculously against the dreary lands surrounding Gloomy Peak. From where Deirdre sat, she could see the rolling hills and waterways of Riverbed. Further out stood Treliave. Deirdre struggled to guess how high she and James had climbed now that she could see the top of the eldestree.

The River Olde vanished beside the Wylde Woods but shimmered back into sight as it stretched out towards Auroval. To Deirdre's left was a gigantic mountain range named the Lower Sleeping Giant. It had always been distant to her, just a distant line to emphasize her horizon. Mr. Raef's story about the Mountain Men made more sense to her now that she was seeing it up close.

Looking towards the spire, Deirdre found its shape to be odd. It stood tall as a tower should, but it had odd offshoots and mismatched lumps all along its sides.

"Ouch!" James yelped. He had shifted his weight backward and pressed the palms of his hands on something hot. Orange embers glowed on the stone behind him.

"Are you alright?" Deirdre called from the rocks below.

"Fine," James lied. He investigated the embers more closely before examining the burn mark on his hand. It was shaped like a paw print — a shadow hound's paw print. After wiping a clump of soot over the hot surface to erase it, James offered his uninjured hand to Deirdre and pulled her up.

"What's wrong with your right hand?" she inquired, having observed that he had helped her up with his left.

James shoved his right hand into his pocket. "Nothing, just a mimblin' sharp stone."

Deirdre tilted her head slightly, but his tone hinted that there was no time for questions. As they hiked on, she noted that James's head twitched at the sound of thunder, and his eyes glanced quickly in every direction before climbing another stretch of steep mountain rock.

James often asked her to wait below while he went to look ahead. Even Biz seemed rather skittish as time passed. It didn't hiccup and squeak with excitement. Nor did it glow when Deirdre patted it softly as she waited for James to beckon her onward.

The final stretch of the climb was the most rigorous. Deirdre's legs shook with exhaustion. The boulders were larger, and their angle was steeper. With Biz's makeshift carrier, Deirdre's instincts for climbing were hindered. She couldn't hop between gaps as James did — not without bonking Biz by accident. For this reason, she had to scoot slowly up and along the Gloomy Peak and destroy the lace and hem of her dress as she went.

They neared the spire. The once looming gray cloud above them now swirled around them as a dark fog. The air tasted of smoke. Deirdre covered her mouth with cloth ripped from James's sleeves. Deirdre had offered to tear more of her own dress, but James wouldn't allow her.

"You don't want to ruin it beyond repair," he said, but Deirdre knew it was past that point.

"What's going on?" she finally asked, seeing him look beyond her right shoulder.

"Nothing," James replied distantly.

"Tell me," she snapped.

James looked towards the spire. They were level with the entrance, but it waited beyond a wide chasm. There was a narrow ledge jutting out along the vertical face of the mountain. It was too narrow to walk across together but wide enough to cross the gap if pressed against the mountain. James was planning what to do next when Deirdre called him by name.

"Do you see that?" James asked and gestured at the ground behind Deirdre. Orange embers glowed on several different boulders.

"What are those?" she asked.

"Shadow hound tracks." He showed her the palm of his right hand. "I've been trying to figure out if it's following us or just hunting nearby."

"Have you spotted it?"

"No, but I've never actually seen one. I saw Biz lift its ears and assumed it was close to us."

Deirdre started glancing around in the same paranoid way as James. "What do you think it looks like?" Imagining was better than guessing.

James's voice dropped, resonating just above a whisper. "It's black, like the shadows in the Wyldar Wood, and larger than any wolf I've seen, and its fur sticks up along the spine." James stood motionless, his lips barely moving. "Its eyes are orange like the embers on the ground…"

"You thought up all of that just now?" Deirdre asked.

James's eyes remained fixed on a point over her shoulder as a wall of fog lifted.

"No. I'm looking at one right now."

Prowling on a ledge above them was a shadow hound. A crescendo of thunder shook the Gloomy Peak. The beast could have swallowed James or her whole in one bite. Deirdre heard it snarl over a low and guttural growl. Magma dripped from a gap between its sharp teeth.

Almost inaudibly, James whispered, "When I say go, run towards the ledge. It's too narrow for it to follow."

"What about you?" Deirdre asked as quietly as she could.

"I'll be right behind," James promised as he gripped the hilt of his sword. Deirdre didn't believe him; she could hear the half-truth in his voice, but there wasn't time to argue. Feeling Biz's warmth against her side, Deirdre gave a slight nod.

"Go!" James shouted before hollering wildly and waving his sword in the air. The shadow hound pounced off its ledge. Sparks flew as it scraped the stone with its claws. The monster barked viciously as it charged.

Thunder boomed again, and Deirdre looked back. James stood between her and the shadow hound with his sword pointed at it. The beast swiped at him with its open jaw. Leaping back, James swung his sword. Deirdre desperately wanted to watch, but Biz let out a warning squeak to remind her that she was running towards a cliff.

James darted from side to side, depriving the shadow hound of a chance to get past him. Its paws burned red. A set of razor-sharp fangs filled its mouth, but the inside of the monster was only impenetrable darkness.

Pressing herself against a wall of stone, Deirdre planted her heels firmly on the narrow ledge. She began to shuffle toward the gigantic doors of the spire.

James slashed at the air, keeping distance between himself and the hound. Eventually, he knew he'd have to turn and run. Thunder continued to shake the Gloomy Peak as a harsher wind began to wail.

Lightning flashed before Deirdre's eyes. She screamed, glancing at the vertical drop waiting beyond her toes.

The monster crouched low, growled angrily, and then pounced. James rolled beneath the beast just in time, knowing he had now positioned it between him and Deirdre. Hot embers burned holes into his shirt. To his relief, he saw Deirdre had crossed the first half of the ledge. The shadow hound rounded on him again. As it charged, James did the only thing he could think of. Swiping his sword against the ground, he sent a wave of hot coals towards the monster. It barked wildly and staggered sideways just as James sprinted past.

Deirdre watched as James made his escape. The shadow hound recovered and tore across the ground after him.

"Hurry!" she yelled as another burst of lightning flashed into the chasm before her.

James tripped on something near the ledge. Deirdre watched as he fell over the edge and into the gap. His sword flew out of his hand just as his other one gripped the ledge Deirdre was standing on. The shadow hound howled, attempting to balance on the ledge too, but the beast was too wide.

"Keep going!" James ordered through gritted teeth. He looked down as his sword crashed against the jagged boulders far below.

"Let me help you," Deirdre shouted back, but they both knew it was useless. The ledge was too narrow to squat on or even lean over without risking her own safety. The thunder boomed again, this time shaking rocks free from the mountainside above.

"Keep going!" James repeated.

Deirdre pulled her eyes away from him to look back towards the tower, but the dark cloud above stole her attention. Purple light flashed rhythmically.

"Don't look up!" James screamed, but his warning was drowned by a clash of thunder.

The clouds began to spiral faster. Deirdre was hypnotized and any courage she had once felt slipped off the ledge and down into the chasm below. All she saw was looming darkness. The wailing winds echoed distantly. Deirdre felt dizzy. She couldn't remember why she was leaning against a wall. She could no longer recall where she was. Her eyes remained locked on the swirling darkness. A figure within it appeared.

Exhaustion from standing on the ledge made Deirdre's legs tremble. With her eyes transfixed, her body began to sway. The darkness reached out to her, extending an arm for her to take. She reached for it. The sensation of falling broke her trance and Deirdre let out a scream…

…but she choked down her voice abruptly as an arm collided with her torso. James had managed to pull himself up with just enough force to knock them both back against the mountainside.

Deirdre's head hit the stone, and she blinked rapidly. James's face came into focus. He had soot smeared across his cheeks and forehead, but he smiled at her weakly and nodded towards the spire. Together they scooted to safety. From across the gap, the shadow hound growled threateningly. It snapped its jaw one final time at them and then vanished into the fog as it fell over them once more.

Though still disoriented, Deirdre could feel James pulling at her arm. She patted her dress and felt Biz still secured inside.

As they reached the tower, James sped ahead and wrapped his hand around a large iron handle. He pulled open one of the doors and hollered at her to get in.

Deirdre didn't need to be told twice. She rushed through the entryway and pulled James through with her. They fell over each other's footing and crashed onto a cold marble floor.

James let out a groan, but Deirdre staggered back to her feet. She reached out for the door, felt her fingers curl around a handle, and then pulled it shut with all her might. The entrance to the spire slammed shut. Instantly, the howling winds and booming thunder fell silent.

-XVIII-

THE SILVER SCEPTER

The inside of the black tower on Gloomy Peak consisted of one large cylindrical room. Antique furniture, chests of clothes, and cobwebbed statues cluttered the space. Dusty, moth-feasted sheets covered objects haphazardly. In the center of the room was a spiraling stone staircase, which stretched up towards the ceiling high above.

As James and Deirdre laid on the floor, a thin, bright ring of light burst from the bottom edge of the spire's wall. It rose steadily higher, illuminating column upon column of intricate tapestries. Almost every brick in the tower walls was covered by them.

Deirdre gasped for breath. Her eyes followed the light as it rose. "What's that light?" she asked.

"A protection enchantment," James exhaled. "Probably to keep the shadow monsters out."

"Did you make it?"

"No." James sat up to look at all the treasure and said, "Probably whoever lived here." He frowned slightly. Nothing seemed to shimmer as he had imagined. "Are you okay?" he then asked Deirdre.

"No," she replied. Flashes of the storm and spiraling clouds continued to trouble her.

"What happened to you on the ledge?" James asked. "You were reaching for something."

Deirdre fought to block the feelings of loneliness. She blinked away a few tears before wiping them with her hands. A mixture of soot and dirt smeared across her face. "I don't know," she answered.

"I'm sorry I brought you on this adventure," James said in earnest. "I knew the woods would be scary, but I never thought…"

"It's okay," Deirdre said quickly. She didn't want James to feel guilty. "We both made it here, didn't we?"

"Yeah," James said slowly. He picked at a burned hole in his shirt.

"Let's find some treasure then!" Deirdre insisted with as much cheer as she could muster.

Together, they got to their feet and wandered into the maze of crates and cloaked objects. Biz floated out of Deirdre's pocket and gave her an endearing lick on her cheek. The wiz was glowing again and babbling incomprehensible Wizzish.

"Where's the bottom of the stairs?" James asked.

"We'll find it," Deirdre replied, but she was already becoming distracted by all the objects surrounding them. She wondered why the Sovereigns of Auroval had hidden all their treasure in such a ghastly place.

James inspected one of the tapestries while Deirdre meandered past artifacts on pedestals and through aisles of books stacked to heights she couldn't reach. Everything had been left in such disarray as if the servants who had brought these items here were terrified to stay any longer than necessary.

Deirdre came across an overturned end table. She stood it back up properly as Biz illuminated its scattered contents. Judging by the layers of dust on the belongings, Deirdre knew the table had been toppled long before she or James had ever arrived. She found buttons on the floor — a whole pile of them. Some were identical to the ones sewn into her stuffed animals' clothes. Spools of shimmering thread revealed themselves to her as she drew nearer. None of this appeared to be treasure. In truth, everything she'd come across so far was rather ordinary.

Not far away, James came across a set of four faceless statues. Propped up against their bases were large portraits with their canvases torn. Feeling for a piece of paper in his back pocket, James then carefully unfolded it in secret:

Don't go back to Bellebrook. Find a staff made from pine in the tower on Gloomy Peak, and bring it to me. I will trade you the real treasure map for it. -V.

James refolded the note and tucked it away. A staff made from pine. There was so much stuff to sift through; it could take him all night just to find it. He wondered if the portraits or statues held any answers. James knelt before one and pinched the torn edges of the portrait back into place. In it he saw a man as old as Mr. Raef with neatly combed coffee-brown hair. A dark eye stared out from the canvas at him. "Creepy," James muttered. He released the painting so that it unfurled and drooped towards the floor.

The statues around him were also useless. He could tell that something, or rather someone, had chiseled away all their distinguishing features. Each of them held an obscure object in their right hand — a sword, a stick, a ball, a crown. None of them held a staff.

"Have you found any treasure yet?" James called out.

"No," she replied. "But I've found something that sort of looks like it."

Deirdre stood before a dozen large wooden chests. Their barreled lids were tilted open. Piled by the thousands inside each chest were small metal tokens. They didn't sparkle like the pirate treasures her father used to tell her about. They were grayish and bland. Deirdre picked one up. On one side of the token, the letter "A" had been pressed. Deirdre turned the coin over. On its back was a tiny etching of a tree. Deirdre picked up another. It was identical to the first. Sifting through a whole layer, she found each and every one of them to be the same. Dropping the token back into its chest, Deirdre moved on.

There were other trunks full of dresses and suits. Boxes of tarnished jewelry. And leather pollen pouches containing odd time-tellers.

Biz floated higher up into the spire and examined the tattered tapestries. No matter how far the wiz went, it made sure to glow bright enough for Deirdre to continue her search for treasure below.

After wiping a wall of cobwebs out of her way, Deirdre came upon a wooden chair carved from a tree stump. Precariously situated on it was an odd statue of a young man sleeping. He leaned against a wooden staff as if he had stopped to have a rest and then never continued on his way.

Ahead of the statue was a long banquet table. Strewn across it were thick tomes and rolled-up scrolls. Rogue pieces of parchment and a detailed moon chart made of tin were held in place by partially melted candles.

Strange markings, which Deirdre couldn't read, danced across the various pages. "I might have found something," she hollered. It wasn't really true, but she wondered if James could translate the mysterious scribblings.

"I'll be there in a minute," James called back. He was staring at a tapestry bordered in purple silk. It contained an image of a treehouse that looked remarkably like his. Even the word Treliave was stitched beneath the detailed embroidery, provoking his interest. But the rest of it made no sense to him.

"Where are you?" Deirdre asked.

"Coming!" James replied. He turned, and with a slight hop, he strolled over to her. On his way, James spotted the sleeping statue. "Did you see him?" He laughed and then poked the figure as if it were a real sleeping man.

"I did. Come look at this."

James didn't move. He scrutinized the stone statue with intrigue. "The other ones didn't have faces."

"The other one's what?"

"Faces, statues," James attempted to explain as he circled the sleeping man. He noticed it held a wooden staff. He wondered if it was made of pine. He gave it a sniff. It didn't smell like much of anything. "Why does he have a face?"

Deirdre sighed. "I don't know," she said. "Maybe this will tell you." She pointed at the page with strange markings.

James stepped away from the statue and leaned over a corner of the table. Biz was too far away to illuminate the paper properly, so James tapped the burnt wick of a candle, and it ignited. A silver spark took the shape of a flame and glowed softly.

"When the night brings fear, and the power of this land has been reclaimed… When the hand draws near, and the rightful heirs have denounced their names — heed caution, those who attempt to wield the Sovereign tools, for hardships will unravel from fate's eternal spool."

"What does that mean?"

James blew out the candle. "It's all Wizzish to me."

"I thought you spoke Wizzish."

"I do."

"So you do understand it?"

"Nope."

Deirdre's brow furrowed. "So you made it up?"

"No, I just translated it."

"From Wizzish."

James shook his head. "No, that's written in Aramayic." He tapped the page. "People say *It's all Wizzish to me* when they don't understand something. I don't understand this poemy-rhyme-thing."

Deirdre did not appreciate James's know-it-all attitude. She watched him walk away from her before she decided to investigate other areas of the tower. Biz quickly drifted back down to her side. "Did you find anything exciting?" she asked it.

Biz hiccupped in response, and although it was, indeed, all Wizzish to her, Deirdre replied and said, "That does sound exciting," and continued on.

James circled back to look at the tapestry Biz had been telling

Deirdre about. The wiz had told her that it was reading the future. Of course, Deirdre didn't understand this. So, while she searched for treasure elsewhere, James studied the hanging cloth. Like the other tapestry he had seen before, this one was also bordered in purple silk. The tapestry depicted an evergreen tree with the word "Raknaan" stitched in bronze beneath it. Perhaps Biz had mixed up one of its words or didn't have the right word in Wizzish to explain what it had read. James scattered his thoughts with a shake of his head.

He moved back to the sleeping statue and poked it again. It was so incredibly life-like that he remained unconvinced that it was just a statue. But the sleeping man didn't stir after James's fifth and sixth poke. And when James took the wooden staff out of the statue's hands, it didn't slump forward.

Nothing happened. James looked at the statue and then back at the staff. He weighed it in his hands. If this was in fact the pine staff Vespra wanted, James had no idea why. She could have found better-crafted ones just about anywhere along the great road. He concluded that he was unimpressed. A boring stick for real treasure and a treasure map was the trade of a lifetime.

"I don't think there's any treasure here," Deirdre said to Biz with a sigh.

The wiz licked her chin and popped.

Deirdre giggled softly.

"Thanks," she told it, and again the wiz licked her chin. "I'm alright," she said. "But after coming all this way, it would have been nice to find some treasure to bring home."

For the first time ever, Biz looked at Deirdre in frustration. Instead of licking her chin, it butted its whole self against her.

Deirdre was forced to look up at the ceiling, and she suddenly remembered the staircase. Cradling the temporarily cross-eyed wiz, she whispered, "You're a clever one, aren't you." She then called out to James. "We haven't searched up there!"

James looked over as renewed excitement dawned across his face. "Of course!" he yelled. Dashing around the room, he tugged Deirdre by the hand and searched for the bottom of the stairs.

"Come on!" he then said when it appeared behind a tall stack of crates.

Together they raced up the steps. Biz zipped ahead, its eyes growing disproportionately wide with excitement.

Even without proof of treasure hiding up above, James knew it was there. If junk was being kept below, then treasure was waiting above. If dingy old rags and ruined statues were left to catch falling dust, then the treasure had to be kept where it could continue to shine. As they raced past more tapestries hung from greater heights, the details stitched within them became more vibrant. But there was no time to pay them attention.

"And here… we… are!" James whooped as they reached the top step. The domed ceiling was directly above them.

Deirdre was temporarily blinded by a mystifying column of light that stretched up from the platform's center. To her left, she spotted a bridge that stretched across the tower. It connected to a small wooden door, which she guessed could lead them to a balcony of some sort. Deirdre peered over the edge of the platform and felt a wave of nausea. It was like looking in the chasm of Gloomy Peak.

"Look," James said in awe. From the ceiling's center, in the heart of the column of light, an object slowly descended towards them.

Deirdre stepped beside him as a thin silver object, no longer than her forearm, glittered into view. The treasure's bulbous top was adorned in tiny diamonds and sapphire gemstones. With the column of light passing through the treasure, dozens of rainbows were refracted around them.

"It's a hammer," James said excitedly.

"A hammer?" Deirdre repeated skeptically. Aside from being top-heavy, this treasure did not look like a hammer.

"Maybe?" James replied, second-guessing himself. "I need a closer look." He stepped into the column of light and reached out to grab the silver object. His fingers slipped through it. The treasure warped like disturbed smoke for a moment before recovering its original form.

James swiped at it again. "Why can't we have it?" he asked her petulantly.

Deirdre sighed as James waved his hand all over the object. It turned into a glittering cloud.

"Well, the Wayfarers said it was a treasure that could be seen, but not touched. They called it a scepter. I think."

"Frazzle-tazzle," James said forcefully. "Ninny-mutton-tutten!" Grasping the pine staff, he swung it at the treasure with all of his might. Like his hand, the staff did nothing.

"Calm down," Deirdre said sternly. She shielded Biz from James's wild swinging. "We just have to give it some more thought." Stepping into the white light to try and retrieve it herself, Deirdre suddenly felt warm and calm. Her mind was freed from all its previous burdens. She kept perfectly still. The treasure was suspended before her. A thought sparked in the depths of her memory. It became glaring and unavoidable. Her father's voice echoed out to her.

"No matter how bad things seem, everything will be alright in the end. If it's not alright, it's not the end," Mr. Heart had once said during a particular bedtime story.

Deirdre refocused her thoughts on the scepter.

"Got anything?" James asked.

"Sort of," Deirdre replied. "Have you ever heard the story about the Sword of Atloria?"

"Nope. What's that?"

"I'm thinking this scepter is that sword. My papa said the sword was bladeless unless it was needed to protect the kingdom." Deirdre stepped back out of the light.

James leaned against his wooden staff. "How does that help us get it?"

"I'm thinking."

Deirdre paced back and forth. "We've come this far. We've fought grumpaguls, escaped Mrs. Doris, outran Wylde roots and shadow hounds… that's it!" Deirdre gasped.

"W-what?" sputtered James with a jerk of interest.

"I know how to get it," Deirdre said. "Or at least I think I know." Moving towards the column of light again, she ushered James to follow her lead. "When we were by the River Olde, you tried to push the leaf in all by yourself. You claimed that you had done it on your own a hundred times."

"I had," James spat defensively.

Deirdre ignored his pride. "You couldn't move it, and I couldn't move it, but together we were able to do it. We started on this adventure together... so in order to end it..."

"We must finish it together!" James grinned sideways and tilted his head in admiration. "How did you come up with that?"

"My father used to say the best heroes and heroines shared the spoils of their adventures. Of course, we aren't bedtime stories, but it's worth a shot."

"Well, there's only one way to find out. Ready?" James exclaimed.

Deirdre nodded. "One..."

"Two..."

"Three," they said together and reached for the scepter. For a moment, the item shivered into smoke, but as Deirdre's hand collided with James's, there was a loud bang and a flash of light. The scepter solidified and dropped heavily into their hands.

"It worked!" Deirdre laughed, leaving the scepter in James's hands.

"Wow," James said under his breath as he stared wide-eyed at the precious treasure. "Hold it!" he nearly squealed while offering it to Deirdre.

"No, you go ahead."

"I'm already holding it. It was your brilliant idea."

Deirdre blushed. "You were the one who brought me on the adventure."

While passing the treasure back and forth, neither of them noticed that the white column of light was fading. They were so wrapped up in their happy argument that they missed the thin ring floating from the top of the spire back down towards the floor. Biz hiccupped and popped, sensing a growing danger. It zipped around them wildly and peered over the edge of the platform.

"Here, you hold it first, but I'll keep it first," James suggested.

"Keep it first?"

"We have to share the spoils."

Deirdre rolled her eyes. "Well, only if I can show it to my parents when I get home."

"Sure," James said as he turned his attention towards the crazed wiz. "What's wrong?"

Biz's fur was no longer glowing. There were no words in Wizzish to describe the perilous trap that had just been triggered. Then the entrance below was blasted to splinters. The protection enchantment was broken.

-XIX-

ESCAPE

The raging storm above Gloomy Peak attacked the spire with all of its frightful might. Black clouds spilled in where the doors had previously been. It swelled, rising like water in a freshly dug well. Then the howling of shadow hounds echoed through the tower. Wooden furniture and old clothes suddenly ignited. Something slimy dripped from above and splattered goo on James's shoes and ankles. Then two more followed. Deirdre looked at one of the black droppings as it began to wiggle.

"Grumpaguls," she groaned. Lifting her gaze towards the ceiling, Deirdre found it to be infested with them. Dozens more began to drop, and some missed the platform altogether and fell into the storm rising below.

"Remember when I told you there was a protection charm on the spire?" James asked, fumbling for the wooden staff.

"Yeah?" Deirdre replied before pulling Biz closer to her.

"I think it was protecting the scepter."

"Then put it back!" Deirdre shouted as thunder shook the tower from within. James laid the scepter on the center of the platform.

Nothing happened. "Stand it up!" she suggested as worry spread in her voice. The grumpaguls were starting to gather and inch towards her. She wished she had brought a bowl of cookie dough or three-tiered chocolate cake.

"It's not working!" James snapped angrily. He shoved the scepter into Deirdre's hand. "We'll have to fight."

"Fight with this?"

"You said it was a sword."

"I guessed it was a sword, but the blade appears when danger is near. I'd say we are definitely in danger, and there's no blade."

James whacked a slug with his staff and sent it flying off the platform.

"Don't they get bigger when you do that?!"

"Sure, but they'll never make it back up the stairs."

Thunder boomed and shook the tower again. A wave of grumpaguls fell free from above. They landed on Deirdre's head and arms. Their ooze felt cold and tacky. She shrieked and swiped them off before clubbing them with the scepter. They swelled to the size of a folisangel.

James leapt in and poked them over the ledge.

Lightning flashed from below. Shadow hounds barked wildly as they ascended the spiraling staircase. James peered over the platform as Deirdre continued stomping and smashing the smaller slugs. He counted nine hounds. Even Biz joined in by offering short bursts of light. It stunned them long enough for James to knock them away.

"There's too many!" Deirdre screamed.

"Get to the bridge," James said while pointing across the platform.

The pack of shadow hounds rounded the top of the stairs. The first one charged straight for James. Swinging the staff, James caught the monster in the snout. It yelped. Biz flew after it and exploded into light. The hound staggered disoriented off the platform and back into the storm below.

Smoke rose from the burning furniture below. Deirdre teetered across the bridge, pushing off grumpaguls as she went. James followed behind her. He shook the end of his staff in warning at the shadow hounds. If they were smarter than grumpaguls, they would know now not to mess with him and Biz.

A particularly wide-mouthed hound stalked towards the bridge. Two more followed. The leading hound pounced at James and caught an end of the staff in its mouth.

"Give it back," James hollered. He shook the staff to rip it free.

The other shadow hounds maneuvered alongside it. James was forced to release his grip on the staff and retreat. "Through the door," He hollered at Deirdre.

"It's locked," she shouted back. "What do we do?"

James looked towards Biz, who had exhausted all its light. The wide-mouthed hound jerked its head to the side and dropped the staff over the bridge's side. All they had left was Deirdre's scepter, which had proven itself to not be a magical sword.

"What do we do?" Deirdre shouted again.

"I'm sorry," James said as his back pressed up against the door. Side by side they stood as the shadow hounds entrapped them.

At that very moment, a beam of emerald light shot through the storm and smoke below. It ricocheted off the ceiling and blasted itself into the center of the platform. Amidst the ear-splitting bang, Deirdre thought she heard someone shout. An explosion of green light turned all the grumpaguls to dust. The shadow hounds were cast off the platform and bridge — away from Deirdre, James, and Biz. Standing where the silver scepter had first been found, now stood a young man holding a staff.

"Which one of you dropped my staff?" the stranger shouted before slamming it into the center of the stone platform. Continuous waves of emerald light radiated out of it, billowing clouds of emerald pollen. It swept over the platform like morning fog moving over a river.

James recognized the stranger immediately as the statue he had taken the staff from. Instinctively, he pointed at Deirdre.

"I did not!" Deirdre gasped. "It was him!"

The stranger rolled his eyes. "Of course it was, you mimblin' maniacs!"

Deirdre and James were ushered aside as the stranger approached the door. He shoved his shoulder against it. "Must be stuck. It's stuck, yes?"

"I think it's locked," Deirdre said. Her attention was caught between the man saving them, his staff spewing clouds of pollen, and the storm now thrashing to pass it.

"Locked?" the stranger laughed. He punched through the solid wood, threaded the rest of his arm through the newly fashioned hole, and pulled a latch from the other side. The door opened.

"Thank you, sir," Deirdre said as she was guided out onto the tower's top.

"Call me Welsh. There's nothing 'sir' about me," the stranger replied.

The sky above was no longer gray. Deirdre peered below and watched as the gloomy storm continued to feed itself into the spire.

"Names," Welsh demanded. He had a funny grin about him as if he already knew this answer.

"James."

"Deirdre."

"Biz," hiccupped the wiz. Its eyes were closed tightly as it sought cover under Deirdre's arm.

Welsh tugged on the cuffs of his sleeves before pointing towards two unmistakably familiar leaves. They were resting gently on the ground, stiff and damp from passing rain. James could tell Treliave had sent them at least a day ago.

"You will take these to safety," he said. "Go home," he added while looking at Deirdre directly. Welsh then turned towards James and knelt on one knee. "Take the second breeze away once you've parted with her." His voice was firm but full of warm intentions. It reminded Deirdre of her father's tone. When James nodded to show he understood, Welsh gave him an affirming grip on the shoulder. "Good, good."

Biz peeped while fighting to keep in Deirdre's shadow.

"Oh, dear," Welsh remarked. He swiftly waved his hand towards Biz and conjured a thick cloud of green pollen to surround it. Palming the wiz and its new cloud like a ball, Welsh then whispered something to it. "Keep to the thicker pines," he told it.

Deirdre watched as Welsh then threw the wiz north off the spire.

"Wait!" she yelled. Her arm was outstretched in a helpless attempt to somehow catch her friend.

"You'll see it again, I'm sure," Welsh told her unapologetically. His attention was now angled back towards the inside of the spire. The storm shook the tower with such force that it was hard to tell if the structure would continue to hold.

"You know how to travel on them, yes?" Welsh confirmed as he looked down at the two eldestleaves.

James nodded.

"Well then, safe travels home." Welsh's eyes fell on Deirdre most heavily as he finished this parting statement. Then after a graceful bow, their rescuer turned on his heels and marched back into the spire.

"Thank you!" Deirdre hollered. The door to the tower slammed shut.

James swore he saw Welsh leap from the bridge through the hole in the door but wasn't sure. "I liked him," he said simply.

"Shouldn't we —"

"Nah, we should do what we're told."

Deirdre felt suddenly perplexed. "Do what we're told?" her temper rose. "Now you want to do what you're told? All this time I've been telling you to take me home, and now — now — now you're ready?"

James smiled stupidly and pointed at the scepter still clutched in Deirdre's hand. "Well, yeah. The adventure's over now, and Treliave sent us these leaves, so she clearly wants us to go home."

Deirdre opened her mouth to shout some more, but she paused. "Who was he?" she asked instead — now that the immediate danger of monsters and storms was gone.

"I don't know," James replied. He extended a hand towards her. "Give me the scepter."

Deirdre handed it to him willingly and watched as he tucked it beneath his belt. She felt odd. With the prospect of going home now within her reach — seeing her mother and father, Pup, Theodore, Woofus, Mr. Button, and Madame Potbelle — Deirdre knew she should have been feeling relieved, or even happy. But Deirdre didn't quite feel either of these things. She didn't feel angry or sad either. The adventure was over, as James had so candidly said, and it made her feel odd.

James pointed towards a maroon leaf, paying little-to-no attention to Deirdre's internal conflict. He explained to her in a hurried manner, "Place your wrist against the stem."

Deirdre did so, and to her surprise, she felt the stem wrap itself securely around her forearm. Her eyes darted towards James's arm to see the same thing happening with his leaf.

"Now grab a fistful of the top corner," James huffed as he stretched his arms out wide.

"And now?"

James snorted and shook his head.

"What?" Deirdre pressed. She hardly thought now was hardly the time for secrets. Without answering her, James stood. He brought his arms closer together, creating a gentle fold in the leaf. Deirdre mimicked him. "What?"

"Trust me," he said to her simply.

A silver aura circled both of Deirdre's hands. She could no longer release either end of the leaf. Before she could utter a confused protest, a gust of wind raced across the top of the tower. Its power was strong enough to lift the eldestleaf and Deirdre with it.

Deirdre screamed. James burst into laughter. Up they soared, away from the Gloomy Peak, leaving all questions about the spire, the stranger, and their adventure behind.

-XX-

PARTING WAYS

Gliding over Riverbed was unlike anything Deirdre could have ever imagined. When she'd first been blown off the tower, the sensation had terrified her. She was a fish out of water. Only James's laugh reassured her that she was safe in the sky. The silver aura around her hands continued to prevent her from releasing the leaf in fear. Deirdre wondered if this had been Treliave's plan all along, and if the eldestree was with her even now.

After James promised for the hundredth time that she would not fall, Deirdre finally began to calm down.

The world seemed so small as it passed beneath her feet. The Wyldar and Wylde Woods were reduced to a cluster of black and green bushes. The River Olde resembled the thin waterway that ran beneath the Pine Bridge in Bellebrook. Tufts of smoke wafted out of chimney tops. The white castle of Auroval shimmered in the setting sun.

"That's Merrivyne and the Great Road," James hollered to her while kicking his feet in the direction of a town topped in red and purple shingles.

Deirdre imagined her father would have loved to travel like this.

She hoped she could retell the experience as well as any good storyteller. Any doubt or fear of being in trouble vanished from Deirdre's mind. She was too excited to tell her parents and Pup about her longer-than-expected journey home.

James tried to see the Gloomy Peak. He twisted and flailed, wanting to know more about Welsh. Why was he no longer a statue? How did he know to rescue them? What intrigued James most, however, was the staff. It was a shame he would no longer get his share of treasure from Vespra, but James reasoned that they still owed him his treasure map for returning Deirdre's mittens.

The wind dipped the children lower towards the ground. Their feet began to skim the tops of tall trees.

"Keep your feet up," James hollered to Deirdre.

The wind had carried her further left. She looked confused, so James raised his knees to his chest as an example.

When Deirdre mimicked James, the wind gave an exhausted sigh and slid the two of them carefully into an open field. The silver auras vanished and the stems uncurled. Looking at the clouds above, Deirdre felt her heart sink slightly. She wished the flight had lasted longer.

James trotted over with the scepter in hand. "Where are we?" he asked.

Deirdre scanned the open field full of hoofprints, carriage tracks, and abandoned wooden stands. "I think this is Marketfair," she told him.

"Where is everyone?"

"I don't know." Deirdre had only ever been to Marketfair in the morning and early afternoon. Seeing the sun now setting behind a distant line of trees, she assumed the caravans of merchants and traders closed their shops before dusk.

"Do you know how to get home from here?" James asked.

Deirdre nodded, looking for a set of trees at the far end of the field. Something metal was forced into her hands. "I can't take this," she stammered when her eyes fell upon the scepter.

"We're sharing it, remember?"

"Yes, but you… your shelf."

James shrugged. "I'll come back soon. You should show it to your parents."

Deirdre beamed. She could already hear the excitement in her father's voice. Rotating it in the fading sunlight, she inquired softly, "You will come back, right?"

"Will you have sugar cubes and tea?"

"Yes." Deirdre laughed with an innocent clearing of her throat.

"Then you can bet I'll be back."

For a moment they stood in silence. The gentle chirping of crickets filled the open air. There wasn't much more to say, now that their adventure was over. Deirdre imagined herself retelling the end of this story to her father. How does it end? She questioned herself. And then, ever so quickly, Deirdre leaned in and kissed James on the cheek.

"YUCK!" he screamed. "WHAT WAS THAT FOR?" He leapt back, scrubbing his face vigorously with both of his hands.

Deirdre was dumbstruck. "What?"

"Why did you put your face on my face?"

"I was saying thank you," she said defensively.

"Well, why didn't you just say it?"

Deirdre fumbled with her thoughts. "Because saying it was too simple."

James groaned. "Get it off me!"

"Get what off?"

"This," James whined. He pointed at the spot where she had kissed him. "It's all slimy and gross. Why is your face slimy?"

Deirdre rolled her eyes and put a hand on her hip. "My face is not slimy."

James collected himself, but his expression remained weirdly contorted. He was blushing and at a loss for reasons why. "You're welcome."

They stared at each other for another moment.

This time Deirdre kept her face to herself. His reaction was not what she had expected. She began rummaging through her shredded dress to find its one real pocket. When her fingers finally found the windstone, Deirdre extended it as an offering to James. "For your shelf at home."

James was overwhelmed with honor. He grabbed it out of her hand and examined it with his same awkwardly contorted face. "Thanks," he finally replied in a gentler tone. The autumn leaves began to rustle as a second breeze announced its arrival.

"This is me," James then announced. He grabbed the stem of her eldestleaf. "You will go home now, right?"

Deirdre smiled. "Of course I'm going home."

"Not on another adventure?"

"Not without you."

James grinned at this. He shoved his new treasure into his back pocket and then grabbed the other end of his leaf. The wind had been waiting for him, stalling impatiently until a silver aura finally appeared around his hands. With a sudden yank, James was flung up into the sky. Deirdre heard a loud whoop of excitement escape James. She shouted her final farewell, and then, just like that, her friend was gone.

Riverbed shrank away as James sailed north. He was puzzled by the wind's choice of direction. Treliave was east of Bellebrook. Nevertheless, he knew better than to question the wind. The storm above the Gloomy Peak was gone, and although James flew near it, the wind quickly jerked him northeast. The sun was half-submerged in the sea.

Then the wind faltered. It dropped James almost carelessly. His stomach bounced up to his throat and then dropped down into its rightful place. The leaf was tugged left, and then dragged down. A rogue tree branch pierced it. James yelped, feeling the leaf release his wrists. Tumbling to the earth, James rolled painfully over gnarled roots and twigs until he came to a halt before a pair of women's shoes.

"Did you lose my note, dearie?" asked Vespra as she stood over him. Her hood cast dark shadows over her eyes.

James rubbed dried pine needles and dirt off of his elbows and knees. He found himself on the edge of an evergreen forest. The face of the Lower Sleeping Giant glowed orange in the last fleeting rays of sunlight.

"No," James replied. He reached into his back pocket for the slip of paper Pahlah had brought him.

"Then where's the staff I requested?" Her voice was sharp.

Behind her stood her companions Match and Laz. Neither of them wore welcoming expressions.

"It's with the statue," James said.

"You didn't retrieve it?"

"I did, but then monsters attacked," James explained. His story quickly turned into inarticulate ramblings with exuberant gestures. "And there were storm clouds trying to eat us, and then the tower was crumbling." He pointed towards the eldestleaf speared by the tree. "We were almost monster food, but then —"

James caught sight of a slender hound-like creature seated behind Laz. "Is that a Rantore?" he gasped with surprise. James had never been up close to one before. They were a rare species with pale silver coats, narrow snouts, and perked ears. The muscles in the Rantore's neck flexed as it cocked its head to look back at James.

"But then what happened," Vespra said as she reclaimed James's field of vision.

"And then the statue came to life. He called himself Welsh."

"Welsh was made flesh again?"

"Do they really know when someone is lying?" James asked Laz as he tried to crawl around Vespra to look at the Rantore once more.

"I thought that might come as a surprise to you," called Welsh from the shadows of the evergreen forest.

Match's hand ignited with flames of purple pollen.

"It does," Vespra answered. She removed her hood. "Finally got the job done, did you?"

"It took longer than expected."

Tapping the staff heavily on the ground, Welsh called upon a wave of emerald pollen to awaken the trees behind him. "You'll be owing me the second half of our bargain."

Vespra shrugged before indicating the openness of their surroundings. "I came ill-prepared."

Roots from the forest began to slither out of the soil.

"But as you are aware, we humble traders take pride in fair business. It would bring misfortune for all if our agreement wasn't kept."

"Cheap words coming from you," Welsh said, void of any inflection.

"Don't blame me for your hard times."

James crept slowly away from the conversation. He tried to get closer still to the Rantore. Between it and a sky serpent, he had always wanted to pet a Rantore. They were the fastest creatures in the world, and apparently truth-tellers as well. The second fact was a myth according to Woodrow, but looking at this Rantore now, James wasn't so sure his friend in Auroval was right. The Rantore sat obediently behind Laz, its discerning eyes following Vespra and Welsh as they spoke. Its whip-like tail flicked only occasionally.

"You won't regain my trust," Welsh snapped. "We will conclude this trade now."

Laz cleared his throat, and Vespra turned her attention back towards James. "It can't be done."

"I've brought you the staff as we originally agreed." The roots twisted restlessly.

"That was then, and it took you a decade to finish the deal. I hadn't anticipated babysitting for that long. If anything, you're in a trading debt for such tardiness," Vespra said calmly. "James, here, is owed a treasure map for completing his quest to return a lost mitten to a precious little girl. Both these dearies are close to my heart. Yet, I fear with this new map of his, James will quickly find himself surrounded by danger. I can't stop him from going, let alone protect him, if I'm to run now to fetch you your sister. So why not tag along on James's treasure hunt and keep him safe for me. You can even keep the staff as a sign of goodwill. I'll bring your sister to you, and we can end the trade on fair terms."

Welsh looked towards James as Lazarus presented him with a long, rolled-up piece of parchment.

Match burned a root as it lashed out at him.

"Shall our trade remain fair?"

Welsh glared at Vespra. "Where does the map lead him?"

"To Evgrenya." Vespra pointed to the staff. "That alone should give the two of you safe passage. Perhaps even some free lodging while you wait for us."

"Why not take me to Amalia now, and then we can all see James's safe passage through the mountain together?"

Vespra grinned. "My time is precious, and it is you who's in a trading debt."

James unrolled the map across the darkening grass with wide eyes of anticipation. His finger found the dotted trail leading through the mountain and into the valley beyond. It hooked right before halting at the "X" he had originally seen three days ago. The word "Raknaan" was inscribed beneath it.

Match, Laz, and the Rantore receded as Vespra and Welsh reaffirmed their arrangement.

Extending her hand, Vespra said, "Until we meet again?"

Welsh chose not to shake on their accord. "Your tricks will blind you someday," he whispered.

"What tricks?" Vespra asked as she pulled her hood back over her head. With a bow and swift turn, she strolled past James without giving him so much as a glance.

The silver scepter weighed heavily in Deirdre's hand as she ran across the broken earth and trapped grass. Dark, towering trees rose in the gathering night, but Deirdre was not afraid. Her excitement carried her to the edge of the glade. She only paused long enough to find the road that led to the pine bridge. A patch of white pompoms and wyldewhites grew along the woodland edge. Deirdre plucked them, thinking of her mother and the smile the blooms would bring her.

A wooden post marked the trail to Bellebrook, and Deirdre followed it into the heart of the forest glen that lay between Marketfair and home. Orange light split between the trees and tangled itself with their many shadows. Nothing appeared off to Deirdre. Nothing seemed wrong.

From up the trail, she spotted the pine bridge's railing as it stretched across the winding waterways. With a multitude of details from her adventure racing through her mind, Deirdre inhaled deeply and merrily declared that it smelled like pine, even though it didn't. The air smelled heavy and dry. Her throat itched with a desire to cough.

Standing in front of the bridge, Deirdre discovered that the center had collapsed. The sight troubled Deirdre, but not enough to stop her from crossing. With a running start and a quick hop, she cleared the gap in the bridge, landing on the other side with a heavy thump.

As Deirdre got closer to Bellebrook, her throat itched with increasing frequency. Floating in the air were the remnants of something foul, like burnt food expelled from an oven. A clearing at the edge of the wood showed Deirdre the way into Bellebrook, but it looked starkly different from what she remembered.

Dark and distorted silhouettes replaced the quaint shingled rooftops and cozy colored homes. The dirt path beneath Deirdre's feet turned to cobblestones coated in soot. Her eyes narrowed as an uncomfortable feeling dropped into the pit of her stomach. She came to the edge of the woods, the final threshold between her adventure and home…

And that was when Deirdre saw that Bellebrook was gone.

Charred frameworks of houses had replaced their once colorful painted facades. The flowerbeds and clean-swept streets were covered in ash and debris — nothing grew. Any sounds of life, whether wild or friendly, were replaced by an eerie silence. Smoke still wafted from smoldering heaps of collapsed rooftops and fallen chimneys.

Deirdre wanted to scream, but a lump in her throat suppressed her voice. She wanted to run home, but her feet could no longer carry her. A desperate need to be held was swelling within her. Deirdre sputtered and coughed as a cold breeze mixed with ash passed over her. She carelessly dropped the scepter and covered her mouth. Bumps rose on her skin as the cold night began to take over the sky.

There was no street post on the corner to indicate Boxton Street. Hardly any houses stood along the block. The residence of Mr. and Mrs. Whitesal remained upright, though it resembled a house of burned cards. A warped accordion lay in the street beside a broken bed frame and toppled chair.

"Mama?" Deirdre called out. It sounded distant and suddenly foreign to her — an echo of a much younger version of herself. Deirdre's mother didn't answer.

The burnt homes still crackled in days-old embers. A whole piano spilled out of a house. "Papa?" quivered Deirdre's voice. The flowers dropped out of her hand.

The silence was painful. Deirdre could feel her pulse in her ears. It thundered so loudly that she almost feared she'd miss her parents calling back for her.

Deirdre waded towards the piano. Her finger pressed down against a key. It clicked. She pressed another one, harder this time. It clicked as well. Desperate to be rid of the pulse in her head, she slammed her left hand over a section of keys. Most of them clattered, but one let out a dying ring, a single parting note that directed her further into the desolation.

Something silver floated over a mound of scorched earth. It had once been a yellow house with black shutters. The studs of a non-existent wall outlined a ghostly living room that no longer housed a plush sofa, a collection of favorite books, or the wicker basket that held logs during frostforth. Deirdre looked for the window where Pup typically sat while waiting for her to come home from the schoolhouse. His paw would have been pressed up against the glass. An inaudible meow would have told Deirdre's parents that she was home.

Walking up the only feature still intact, the front stone steps, Deirdre found a tarnished door number 6. It was mangled and partially buried in ash.

Deirdre moved helplessly into the wreckage, walking steadily towards the center of the debris. Her breathing was shallow. She half-hopefully expected to see the backyard resting normally just beyond the mound — a garden, a flowerpot, her mother's favorite bench. None of it remained. Deirdre stood inside the empty plot and looked down.

The only hint that her home had ever existed remained in the soot-smeared ear of a stuffed rabbit. There was no pig. There was no dog. There was no teddy bear. There were no teacups or paper doilies.

Deirdre stared at the rabbit's ear for a long while. She looked at the batting used to stuff it as it quivered in the evening breeze. She looked at the burnt edges, the cauterized tip, but she did not touch it. Then, as the sun truly abandoned Deirdre, a silver glow reminded her that something else was still there.

Hovering above her, just within reach of her fingertips, was a letter wrapped in silver pollen. And like the rabbit ear, Deirdre stared at it. It turned aimlessly, as if unable to commit to a direction. She knew it was waiting to be taken. Her letter had reached its destination, but it too had nowhere else to go. Carefully, Deirdre raised her hand and felt the warmth of the pollen pass through her fingers. She plucked her letter from its holding place and the pollen dissolved, leaving Deirdre cold and alone in the dark.

TO BE CONTINUED…

The Skyrunner's Captain

~Tales from Elderland~

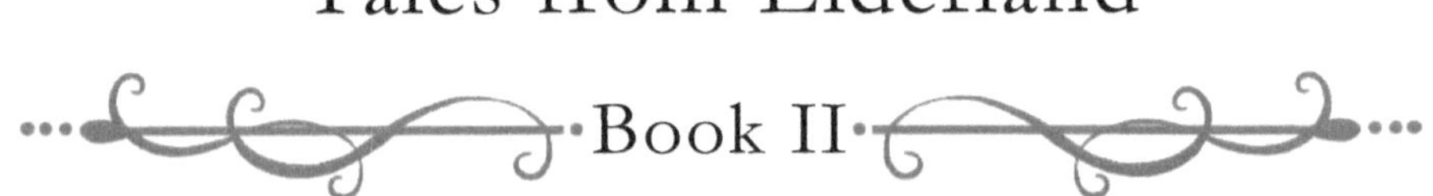

Book II

THE EXOTIC POT

The briny air clung to the cold as it washed up from the Aramayus. Crowds of bundled-up people huddled together as they roamed the dirt-trodden paths of Marketfair. With Frostforth announcing its presence, the gathering of caravans and merchants became more like the trees — bare and still beneath a cheerless gray sky. Bonfires built along the road drew more people over than the items presented for sale at merchant stands. Only the essentials were bought. Many merchants had chosen to travel south towards Little Rock in the Southern Isle, where better business was promised. Once the leaves had fallen around Marketfair, the shouting and bargaining dwindled. Most people near the trading grounds blamed the cold for Marketfair's lack of cheer. However, with Marketfair's relocation to the bay and the new law requiring merchants to possess Trader's Papers in Elderland, much of the true charm at Marketfair had been lost.

Instead of seeing Wayfarer caravans with brightly painted carriages, there were iceboxes full of fish. Where once there were smells of Southern Isle perfumes, cured meats, spices, and incense, now there was the scent of salt and wet stone. The Reunification Act of Elderland had limited the Wayfarers' presence in the trading grounds.

Roadside sales were forbidden. Every trader had to own a shop in one of the towns or had to pay for papers that allowed them to sell on camping grounds. Caravans could not congregate in settlements. They were limited to four carriages per party.

A white tent enclosed on all sides stood off the mainline of vending carts and shops. The entrance flap folded as a customer pushed their way inside. Smoke and a bitter sea breeze followed in from the road.

"You came at just the right time. We'll be closing soon," Amalia said.

The customer, who was heavily bundled, nodded silently. His face was wrapped in scarves and masked in shadows from a hood drawn over his head. All that could be seen were his eyes and the flesh scarred beneath them.

Amalia's fire-red curls bobbed up and down in a bunch that was tied together by a lilyvine. She had soft features, with freckles that surrounded a pair of dimples she felt too old to have. Her guardian and friend, Laz, often told her that they highlighted her smile. Yet, Amalia felt her smile was always overlooked because of her right foot. It was twisted, and the leg attached to it had grown stiff. She had a faint memory of jumping off rocks, but it was a murky memory from when she was only two or three. No one knew the story of how Amalia had come to break her leg, only that it could not be fixed.

"Can I interest you in buying some white pom-poms or frost-tipped lavender?" All the tables under the tent were lined with potted herbs and flowers.

"Laz, please," wheezed the customer.

"Pardon?" Amalia watched him eye the back of her tent.

"I would like to trade with Laz." Reaching into several layers of coats and pockets, the stranger revealed a small, corked vial containing emerald eldestree pollen.

The entrance to the tent flipped open, and as another guest entered, Amalia masked her fear. Could it be a Unity Keeper? Her cheeks burned hot, but only for a second. The new guest was just a young woman with blonde hair and a jacket that could be worn by a wealthy fisherman of Blaemede. Amalia and her friend Laz did not have Trader's Papers. Looking back at the man, Amalia noted that the vial had already been re-pocketed.

"An herbal tent?" the new guest remarked with disappointment.

"The best in Elderland," Amalia returned quickly. Her voice was chipper with a song-birdish tone that rang well to the ears of someone with pence. "Welcome to the Exotic Pot, Miss…"

"Leah," she replied and said nothing more. She stared at the flowers absently. Like so many other guests, she had entered the unmarked tent with the hopes of finding something interesting — things that only Wayfarers sold in secret.

"Laz," the man grumbled again.

Amalia nodded, and while keeping her eye on the younger customer, she reached for a bell beneath the table. It chimed twice. Leah looked up curiously. "Just calling for another friend," Amalia explained to her. For a second time, the young guest looked back to the flowers.

"I knew you would be here in time, Niko!" Laz declared. A tall, dark-skinned man appeared. He was well dressed in vibrant lavender silks. His presence alone brought a feeling of life to the quiet tent.

"Miraculous, how you always seem to know," Niko returned. His words were strained by a shortness of breath. Amalia now recognized the customer and understood why he kept himself wrapped in cloth up to his eyes.

"You will be interested in Harvesting Hill weeds, yes?" Laz asked as he glided through the tent. His baritone voice and Southern Isle accent caught Leah's attention.

"Let me help you find something," Amalia said to her.

Leah looked at Amalia's crutch and answered, "I'm just passing the time."

"Well, let me help you pass more of it." Amalia offered a smile. The customer reminded her of someone she was close to, another Wayfarer.

"That's alright. I should probably be leaving."

"You're waiting on someone, yes?" Amalia stepped to keep in eye contact. "Stay here and keep warm. There's no point waiting outside for them. The bonfires are crowded." Amalia let Leah contemplate for a moment before adding, "I'll read your palm for an iron pence."

Leah's attention was caught. "So, you are a Wayfarer," she whispered, as if merely by mentioning the word, she would get in all sorts of trouble.

"No," Amalia answered. "But as a traveling florist, you can pick up a thing or two." Pointing towards a pot of parchleaves, she added, "Those only grow in Little Rock by sky serpent nests." She pointed towards another pot. "And those only grow east of Auroval. They bloom only under the first few nights of Heatspell."

Leah eyed the parchleaves with excitement. "So, you know Wayfarers?"

"Dozens," Amalia replied before taking Leah's palm into her own.

"Niko, are you sure I can't interest you in buying something from the Harvesting Hills?" Laz asked as he discreetly uncapped the bottom of a small flowerpot. The bottom piece revealed a secret tray of silver eldestree pollen.

Niko shook his head. "I need Little Rock herbs, for tea."

Lazarus reached for a small cup that held a single sprout. He kept it low and close between them so other eyes could not see, then he uncapped it to reveal just a pinch of purple eldestree pollen.

"That's it?"

"The road is long to Little Rock, and longer back."

"Fine," Niko wheezed. He removed his vile of emerald pollen. "Doubt you'll want to bring a scale in view," he said softly. "Besides, you're getting more out of this bargain than I am." He pressed the vial down into the soil of a flowerpot between them and moved dirt over the top to conceal it.

Laz extended the sprout. "I'll be in your debt until next time."

Niko snorted at this and hobbled out of the tent. Then as Laz removed the evidence of their trade, the tent flap opened a third time. A stronger cold surged into the room. "How may we be of service to you?" Laz asked calmly as a woman dressed in thick red robes entered. A sword was strapped to her side. It bore the sigil of Auroval.

"Registration check," she barked. "Show me your Trader's Papers."

Amalia quickly removed her hand from Leah's palm and smiled.

Laz nodded. "I keep them in the back. Stay here for a moment."

"Leave that," the Unity Keeper ordered while indicating the flowerpot in Laz's hands.

Knowing what had been buried beneath the soil, Amalia quickly answered, "It's a delicate flower from the Southern Isle. This tent is too cold for it to stay out any longer. We need to keep it warm in the back tent."

"Yes," Laz said. "If that is a problem, you may follow me back there."

Leah, who had grown nervous in the presence of the woman, tried to inch away. "Come back with the documents," the woman said to Laz. In the blink of an eye, her hand then shot out and grabbed Leah by the arm. "Where are you going?"

"To meet my father," she squeaked.

"How old are you?"

"Sixteen."

The Unity Keeper moved Leah into the center of the tent where a single candle-lit lantern offered light. She gave her blonde hair a tug and examined the roots. "Who are you traveling with?"

"My father."

"Where are you coming from?"

"Blaemede." Tears were streaking down her cheeks by the time Amalia stepped in.

"You're hurting my business."

"I could be saving your business," the Unity Keeper returned. She reached to her side and removed a scroll. "Last night there was an attack on the Great Road. The Farwood Thief was spotted again, and this time, the victims were able to give a description — a young girl with blonde hair."

Amalia looked towards Leah, knowing all too well that she was not the Farwood Thief. "There must be a hundred girls with blonde hair from here to Merrivyne. How can you judge on such a vague description?"

The Keeper began examining Leah's bundled jacket. She was searching for something specific and knew almost instantly that it was not there. Amalia feared the Keeper would stay, that she would wait to see the Trader's Papers, which Laz didn't have. They would be arrested on the spot. Their tent would be searched from top to bottom, and when the Unity Keeper found hidden eldestree pollen in the base of every flowerpot, she and Laz would be sent off to the prison in Auroval.

Amalia shivered at the thought of the rumors she had heard.

Unlicensed traders, mostly Wayfarers, who broke the new laws were tossed in a metal cage surrounded by stone walls kept far beneath the city streets.

At that moment Laz returned with a small scroll rolled up in his hand. "What is the meaning of this?"

The Unity Keeper released Leah but kept her from exiting the tent. "Eight-hundred iron pence was stolen last night from a forge delivery heading towards Blaemede. The criminal proclaimed herself to be the Farwood Thief and was described by the carry-men as a young girl with blonde hair, a knife, and a Wayfarer's pollen pouch." The woman surveyed the tent with her suspicions.

"That is a great story," Laz returned, "but you came in here for papers. Not to bully young women. Now let her leave or follow her back to whomever she's with." He waved the scroll in his hand and pointed towards the tent flaps. The Keeper glanced towards the papers in his hand before letting the young woman exit.

"I'll be back to see those," she promised. Then she left the tent to confirm Leah's father was nearby.

"I didn't know we had Trader's Papers," Amalia said, letting out a breath.

"We don't," Laz said quietly with a grin. He pulled the scroll open to reveal a blank piece of parchment. "Match found the papermill that prints them and bought a few blank sheets. We've kept them on us for a moment like this. Now quick, let's pack up before she returns."

Reaching into a deep pocket, Laz pulled a handful of silver pollen-free and tossed it into the air. He called it to help sort the flowerpots onto trays. Amalia did the same, guiding them with a wave of her hand to a wagon just behind their tent. The Exotic Pot's traveling shop was dismantled within minutes. By the time the Keeper returned to examine the Trader's Paper, Amalia and Laz were far from Marketfair and common sight.

BOOKS BY J.D. MANKOWSKI

The Tales from Elderland Series

The Silver Scepter

The Skyrunner's Captain

The Stone King

The Dream Weaver's Fate (Coming Soon)

OTHER WORKS

Blood in the Gray – A Kindle Vella Series

Coven Ascending – An Ash Fall's Universe Novel

A Wealth of Knowledge – An 'Of Metal & Magic' Novella

**Learn more about the author and books, by visiting
www.jdmankowski.store**

ABOUT THE AUTHOR

J.D.'s professional career as an author began with the 2015 printing of his coming-of-age fantasy series *The Silver Scepter* followed by its sequel *The Skyrunner's Captain*.

Since then, J.D. has been published in collaborative story universes such as 'Of Metal & Magic' and 'Ash Falls'. He has also had short stories featured in anthology collections: 'Rivers of Ink: Literary Reflections on the Penobscot' and 'Grifty Shades of Fey'.

His ongoing serial fiction series about pirates 'Blood in the Gray' has been ranked among the top 25 Kindle Vella stories on multiple occasions.

J.D. lives in Maine with his wife and three cats.